The Grapl ... 2009

SNOW WHITE

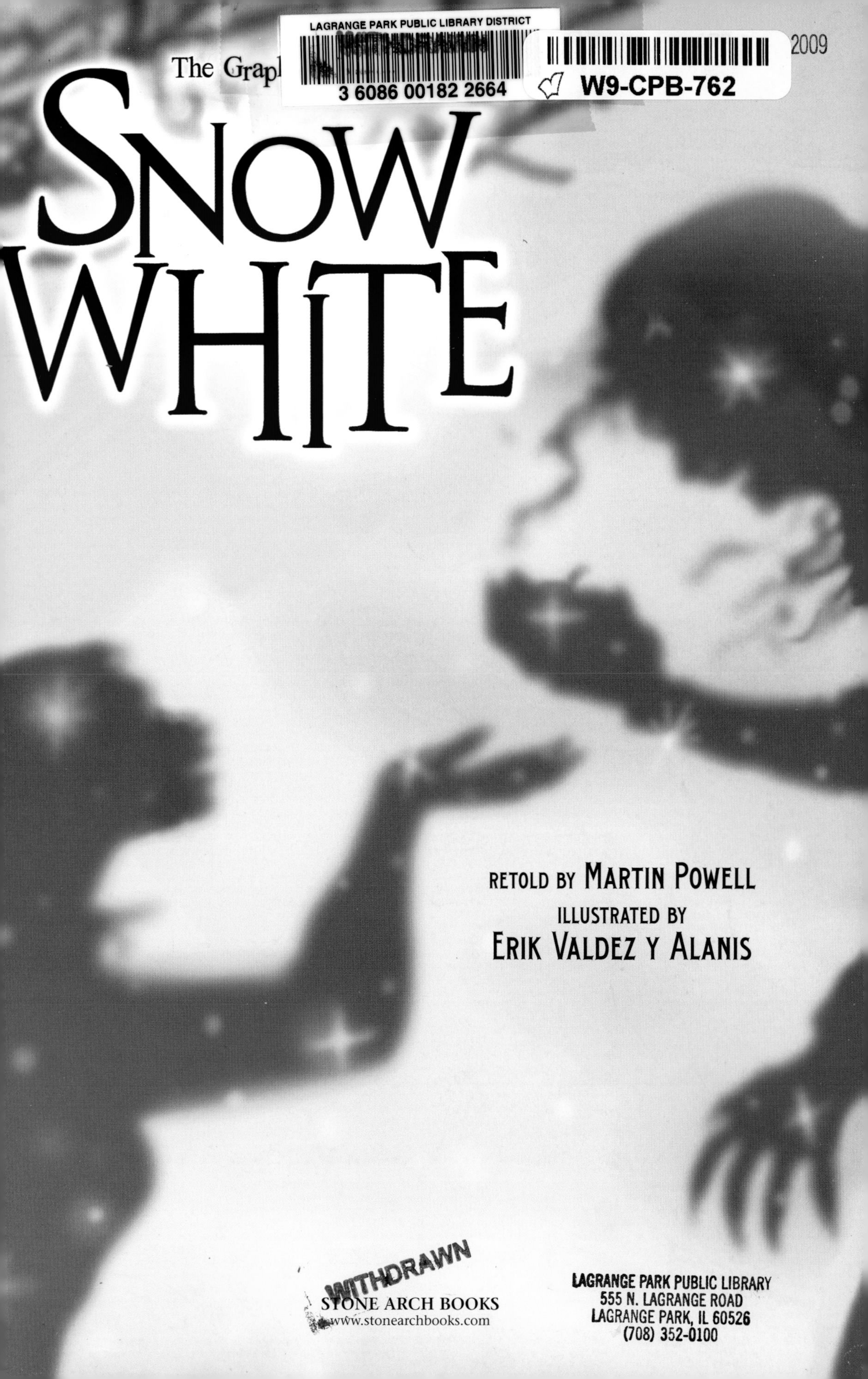

RETOLD BY MARTIN POWELL
ILLUSTRATED BY
ERIK VALDEZ Y ALANIS

STONE ARCH BOOKS
www.stonearchbooks.com

Graphic Spin is published by Stone Arch Books
151 Good Counsel Drive, P.O. Box 669
Mankato, Minnesota 56002
www.stonearchbooks.com

Library of Congress Cataloging-in-Publication Data
Powell, Martin.
   Snow White / by Martin Powell; illustrated by Erik Valdez y Alanis.
   p. cm. — (Graphic Spin)
   ISBN 978-1-4342-1192-7 (library binding)
   ISBN 978-1-4342-1394-5 (pbk.)
   1. Graphic novels. [1. Graphic novels. 2. Fairy tales. 3. Folklore—Germany.] I. Valdez y Alanis,
Erik, ill. II. Snow White and the seven dwarfs. English. III. Title.
PZ7.7.P69Sn 2009
741.5'973—dc22   2008032049

Summary: Once upon a time, an evil queen possessed a powerful mirror. It spoke only the truth,
which often pleased the queen. But when the mirror reveals that the queen is no longer the fairest
lady in the land, her heart grows cold. She seeks revenge against the beautiful maiden, vowing to
destroy the lovely Snow White.

Creative Director: Heather Kindseth
Designer: Brann Garvey

1 2 3 4 5 6 14 13 12 11 10 09

Printed in the United States of America

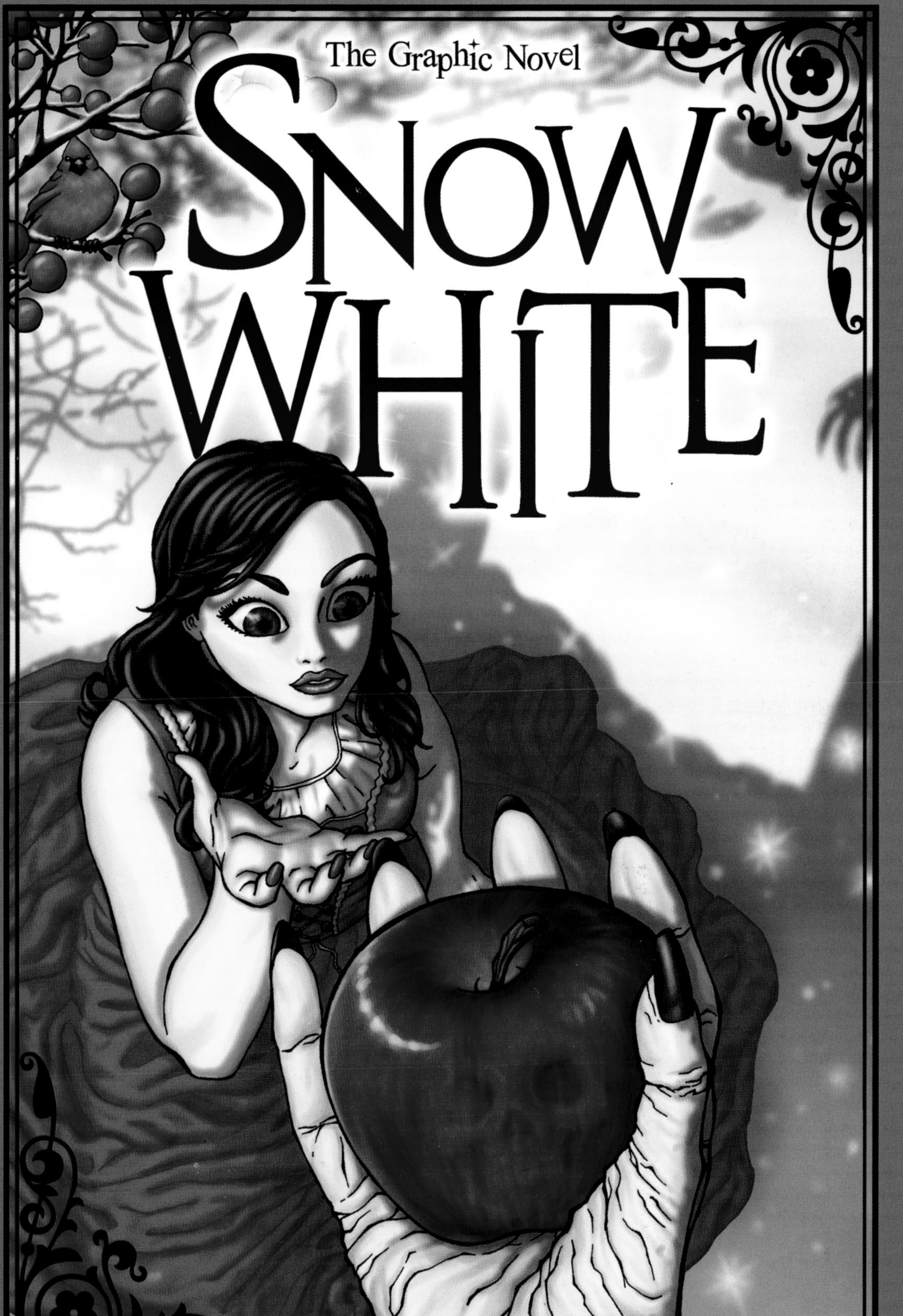
The Graphic Novel
SNOW WHITE

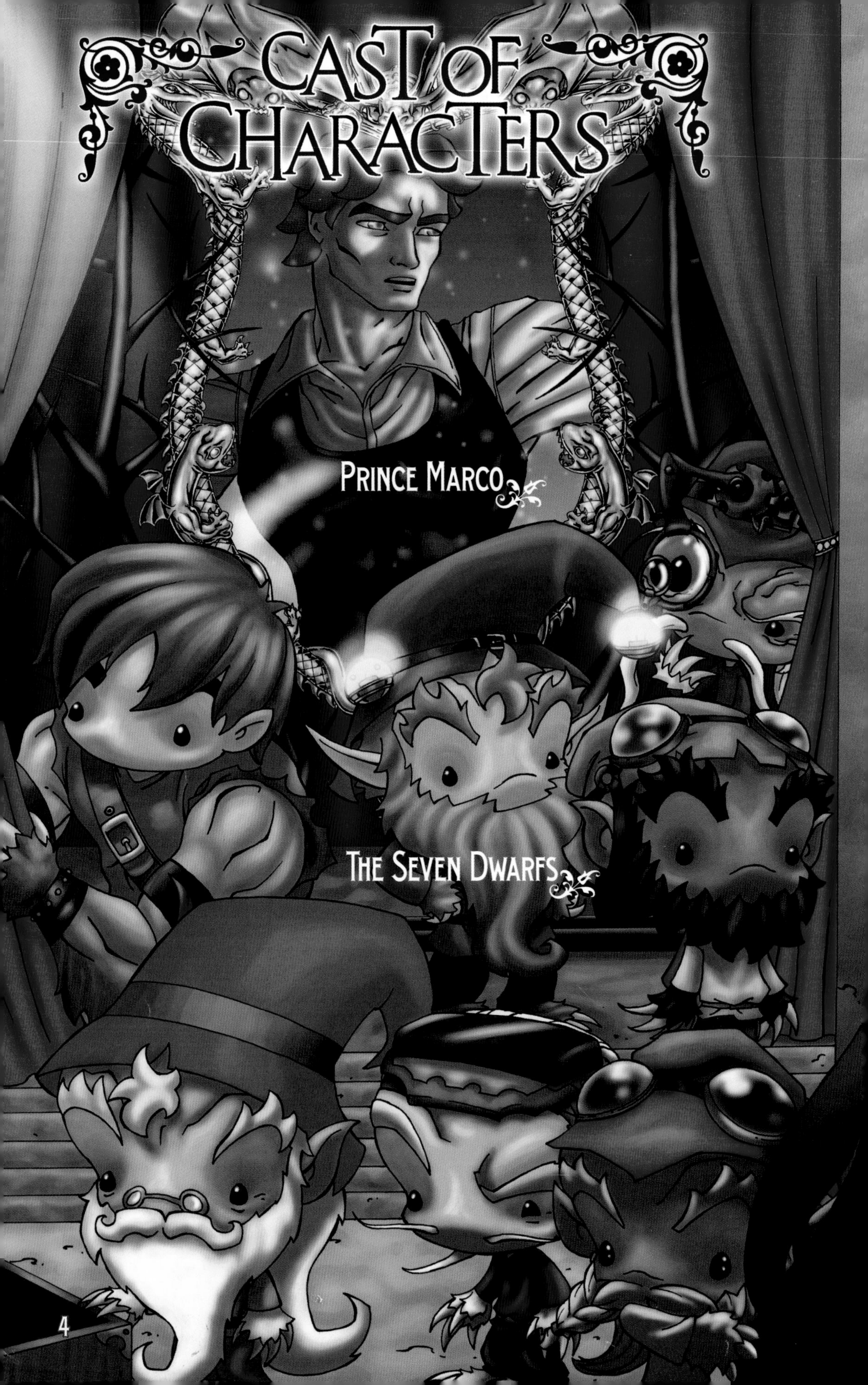
CAST OF CHARACTERS
PRINCE MARCO
THE SEVEN DWARFS

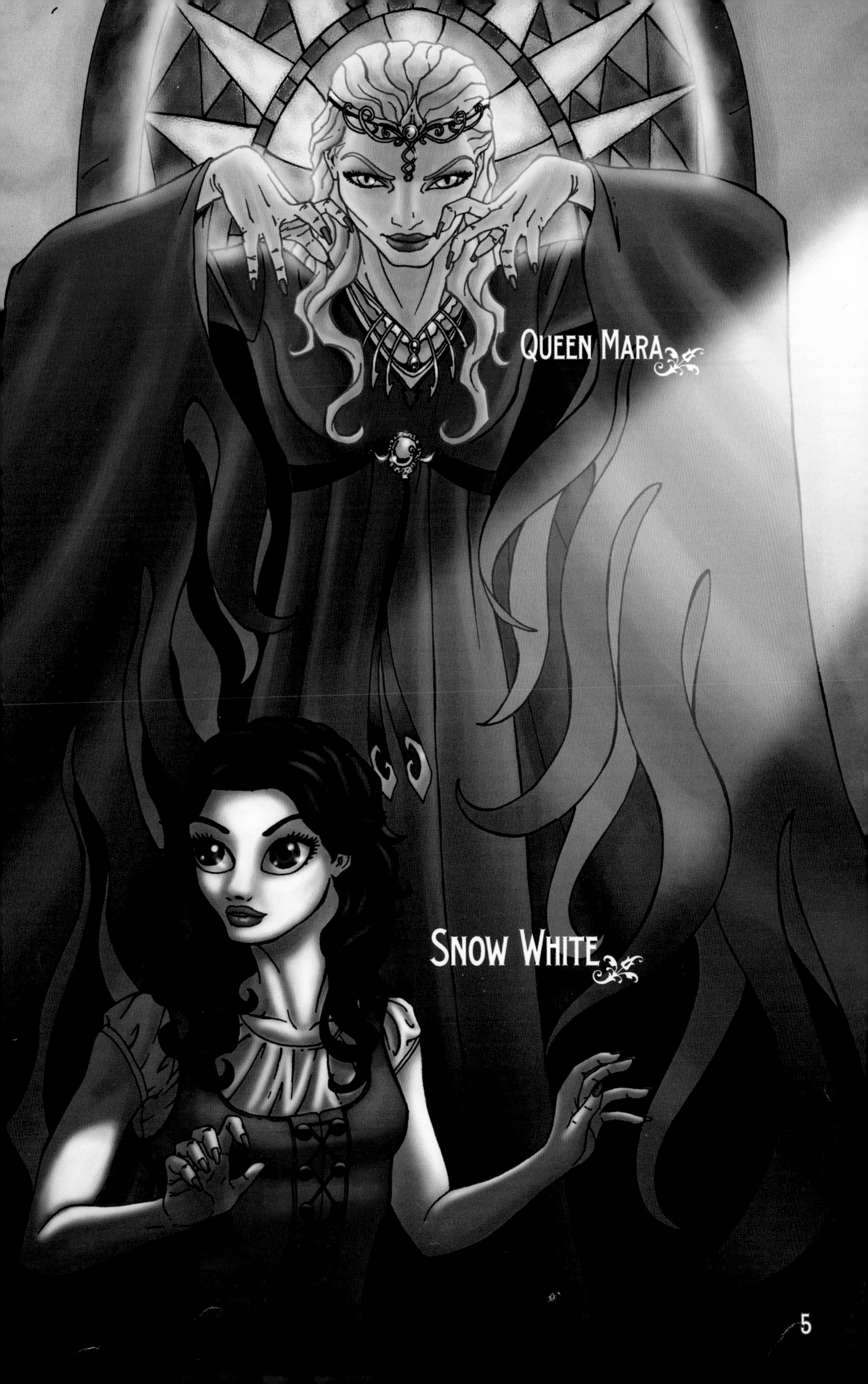
QUEEN MARA
SNOW WHITE

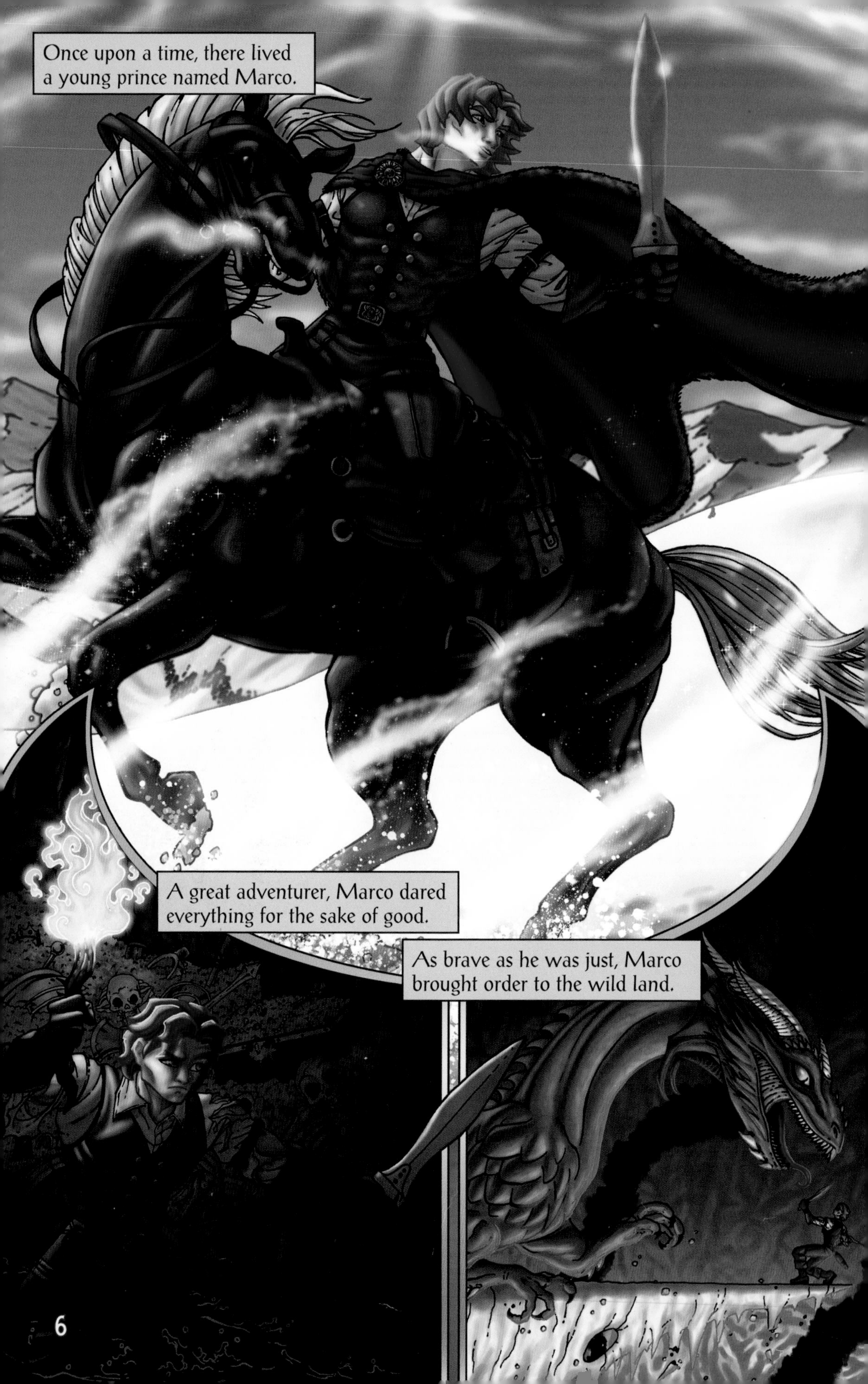
Once upon a time, there lived a young prince named Marco.
A great adventurer, Marco dared everything for the sake of good.
As brave as he was just, Marco brought order to the wild land.

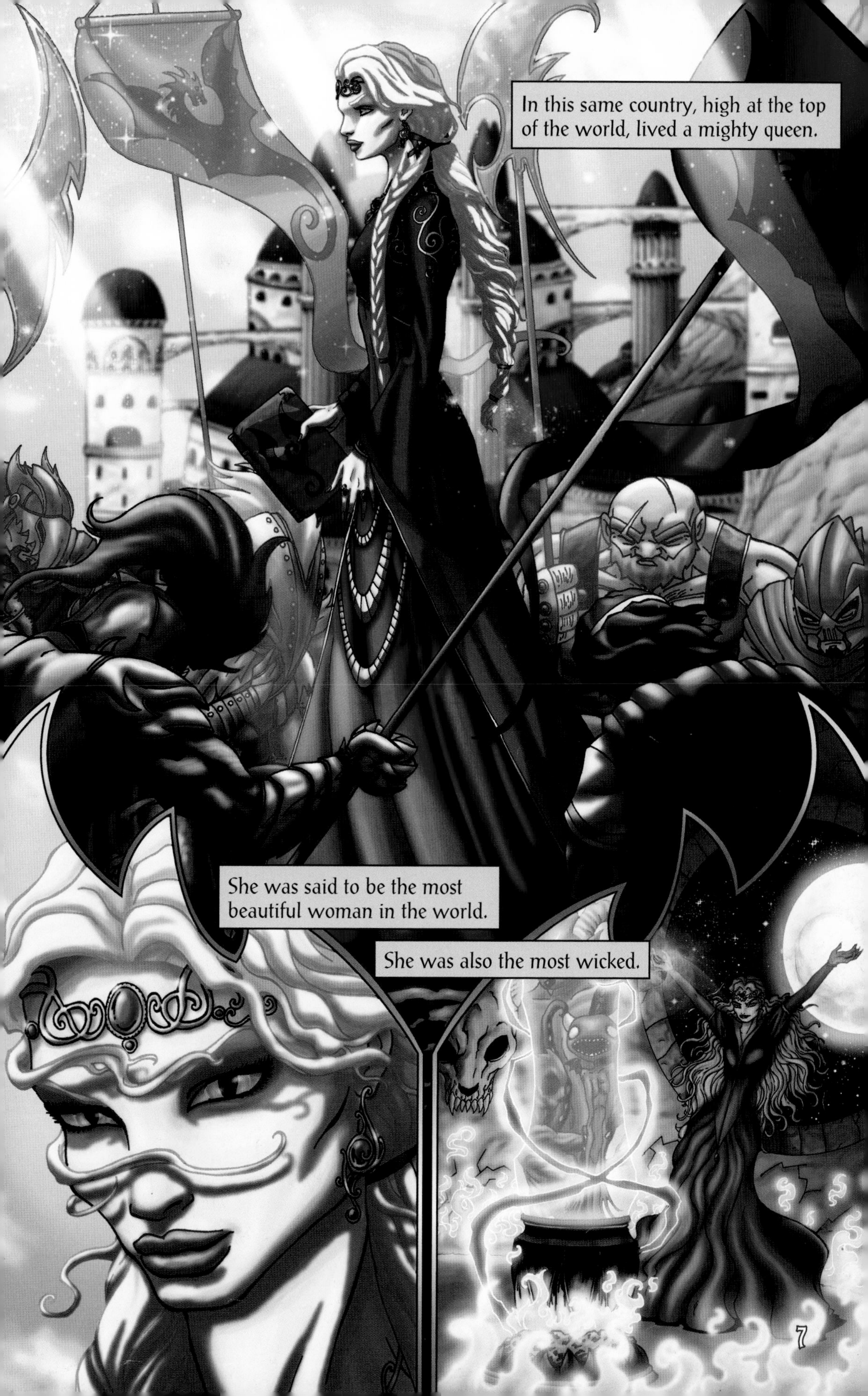
In this same country, high at the top of the world, lived a mighty queen.
She was said to be the most beautiful woman in the world.
She was also the most wicked.

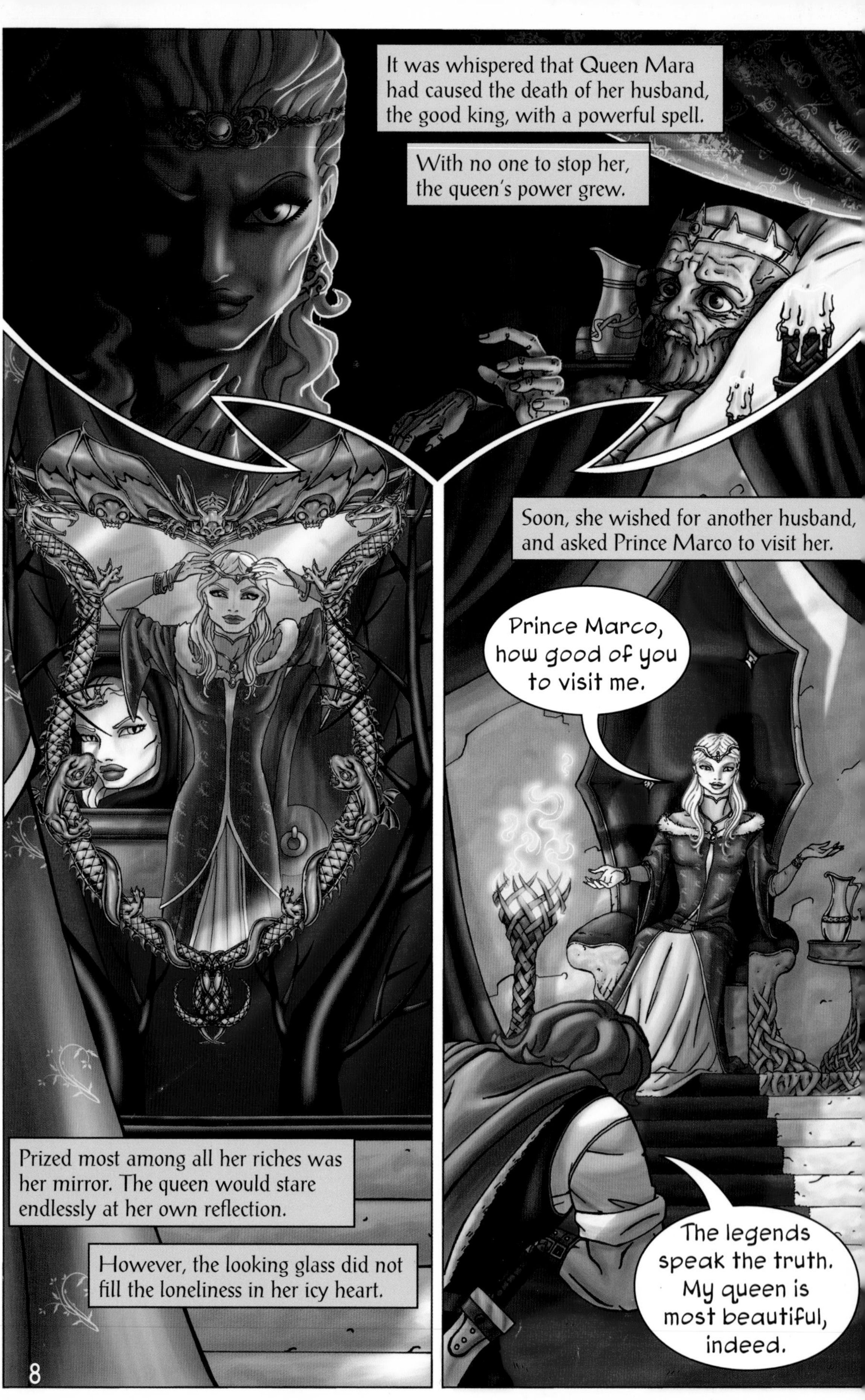

It was whispered that Queen Mara had caused the death of her husband, the good king, with a powerful spell.
With no one to stop her, the queen's power grew.
Prized most among all her riches was her mirror. The queen would stare endlessly at her own reflection.
However, the looking glass did not fill the loneliness in her icy heart.
Soon, she wished for another husband, and asked Prince Marco to visit her.
Prince Marco, how good of you to visit me.
The legends speak the truth. My queen is most beautiful, indeed.

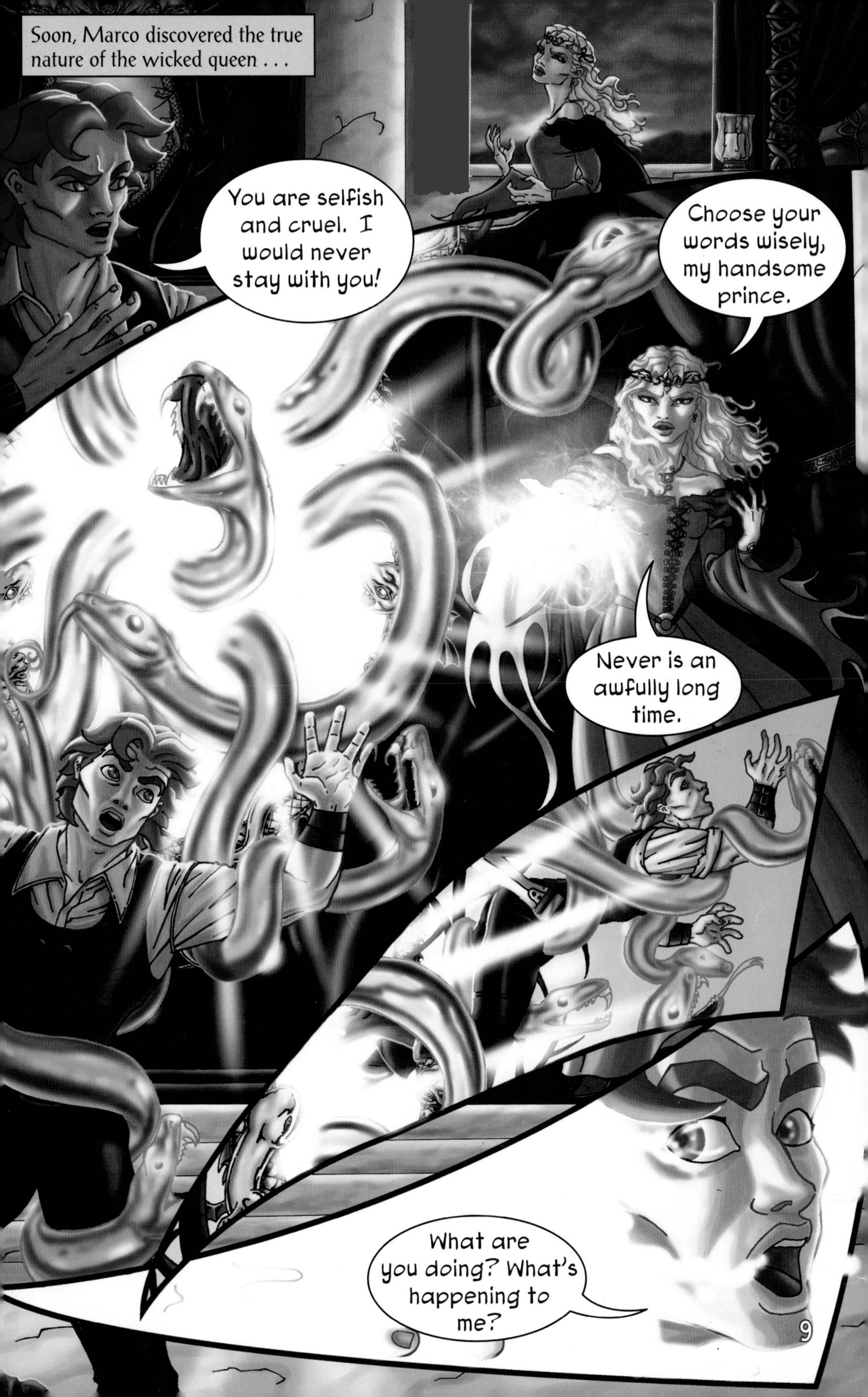
Soon, Marco discovered the true nature of the wicked queen . . .
You are selfish and cruel. I would never stay with you!
Choose your words wisely, my handsome prince.
Never is an awfully long time.
What are you doing? What's happening to me?

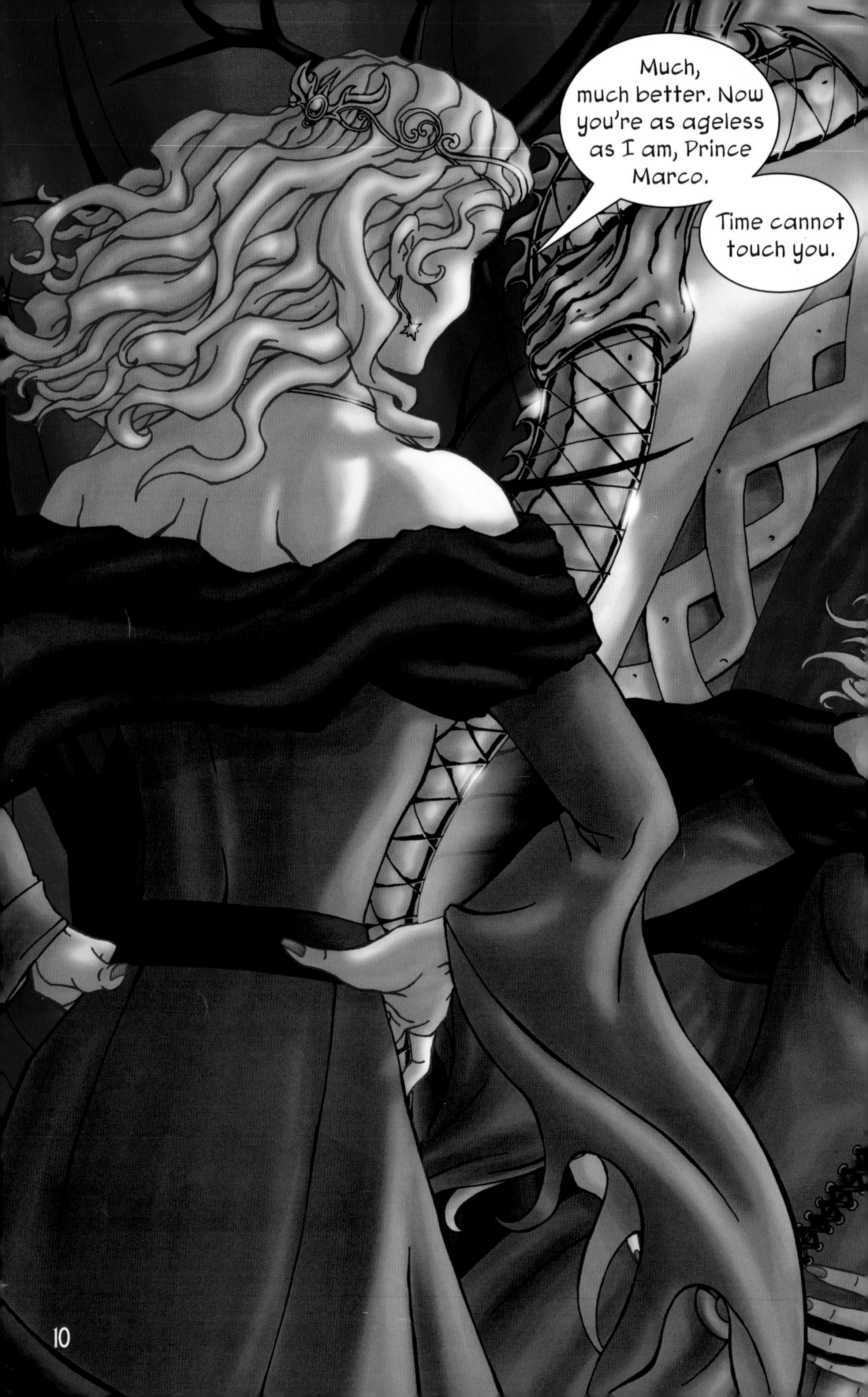
Much, much better. Now you're as ageless as I am, Prince Marco.
Time cannot touch you.

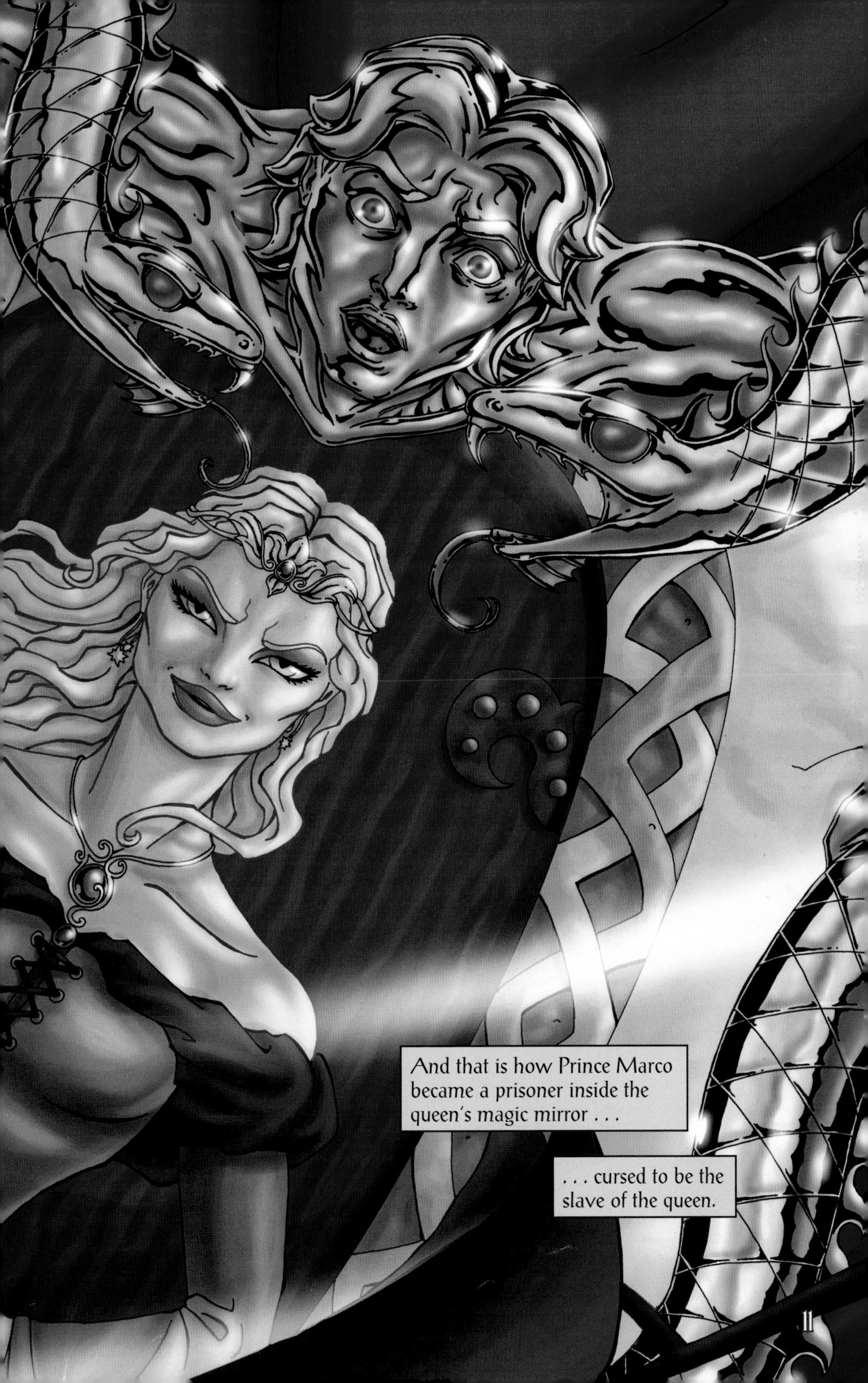
And that is how Prince Marco became a prisoner inside the queen's magic mirror . . .
. . . cursed to be the slave of the queen.

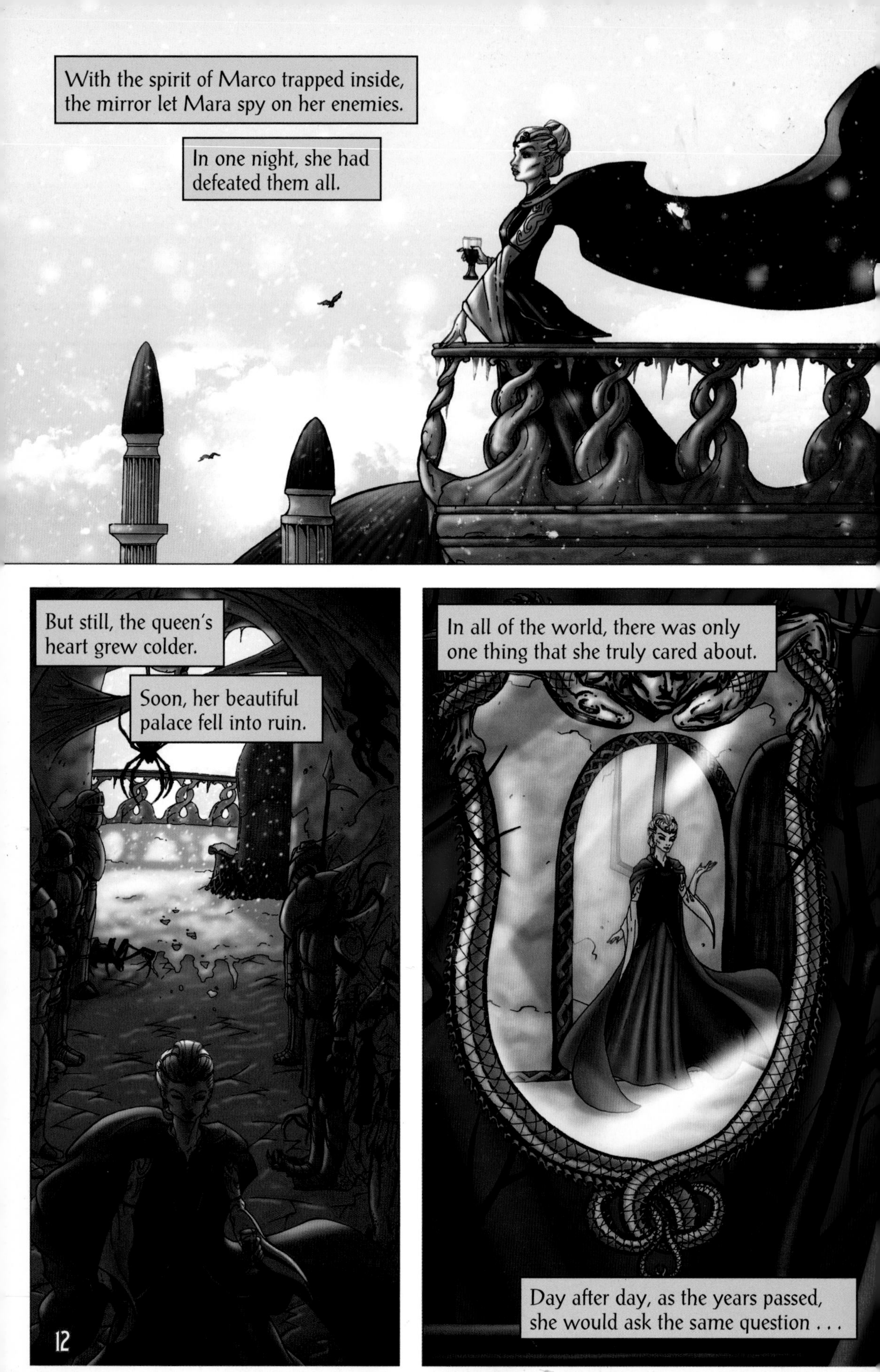
With the spirit of Marco trapped inside, the mirror let Mara spy on her enemies.
In one night, she had defeated them all.
But still, the queen's heart grew colder.
Soon, her beautiful palace fell into ruin.
In all of the world, there was only one thing that she truly cared about.
Day after day, as the years passed, she would ask the same question . . .

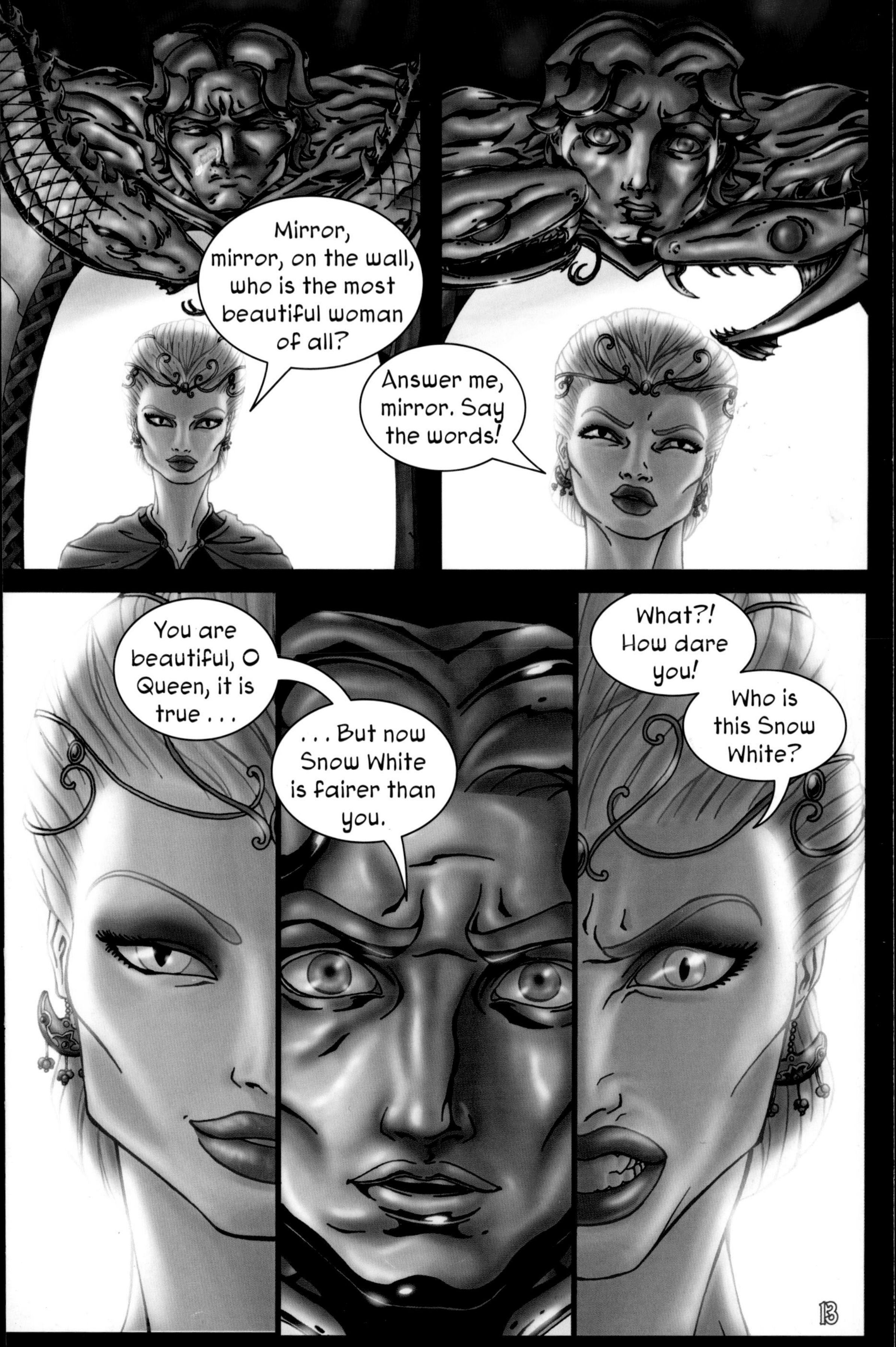
Mirror, mirror, on the wall, who is the most beautiful woman of all?
Answer me, mirror. Say the words!
You are beautiful, O Queen, it is true . . .
. . . But now Snow White is fairer than you.
What?! How dare you!
Who is this Snow White?

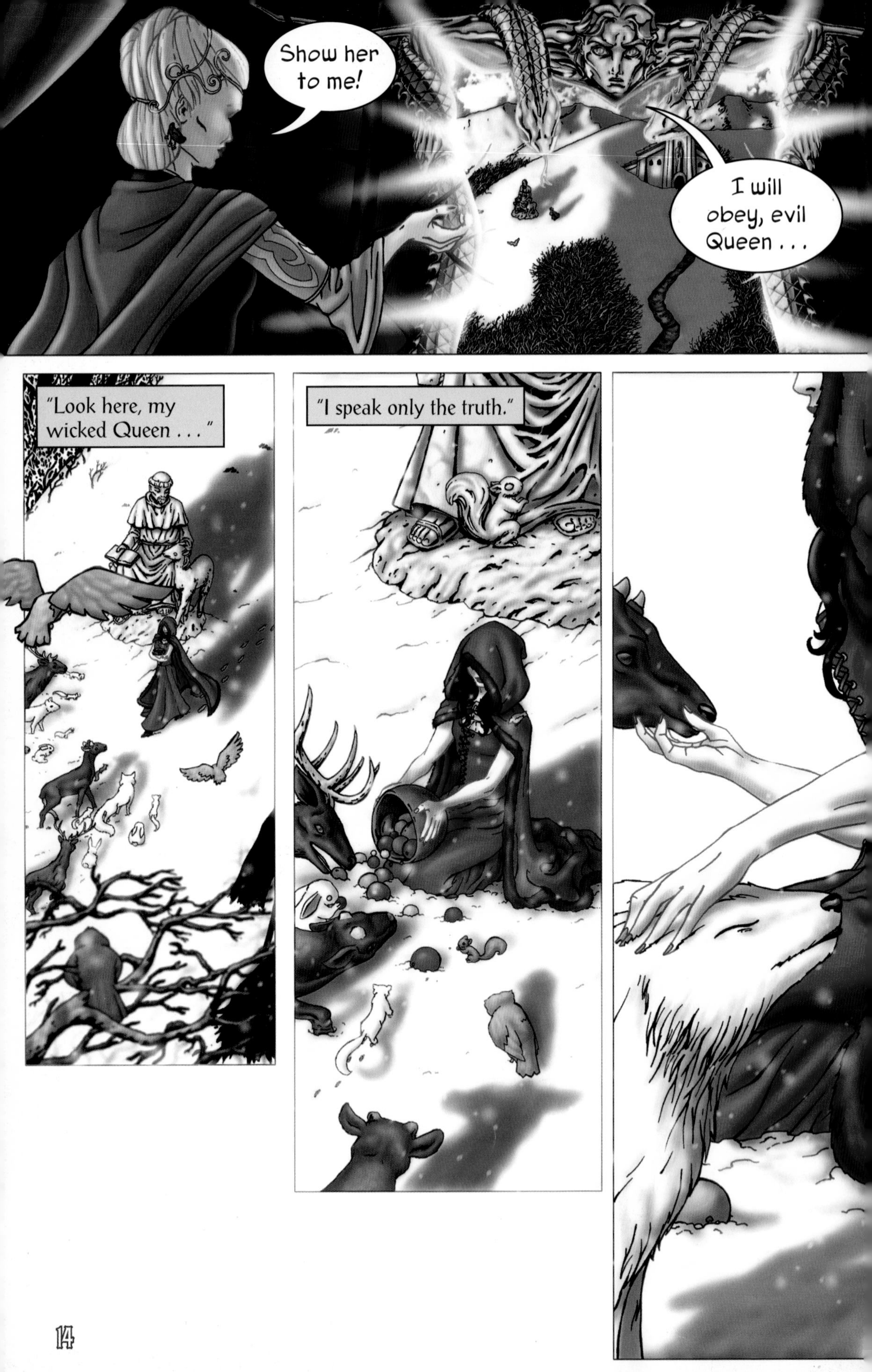
Show her to me!
I will obey, evil Queen . . .
"Look here, my wicked Queen . . . "
"I speak only the truth."

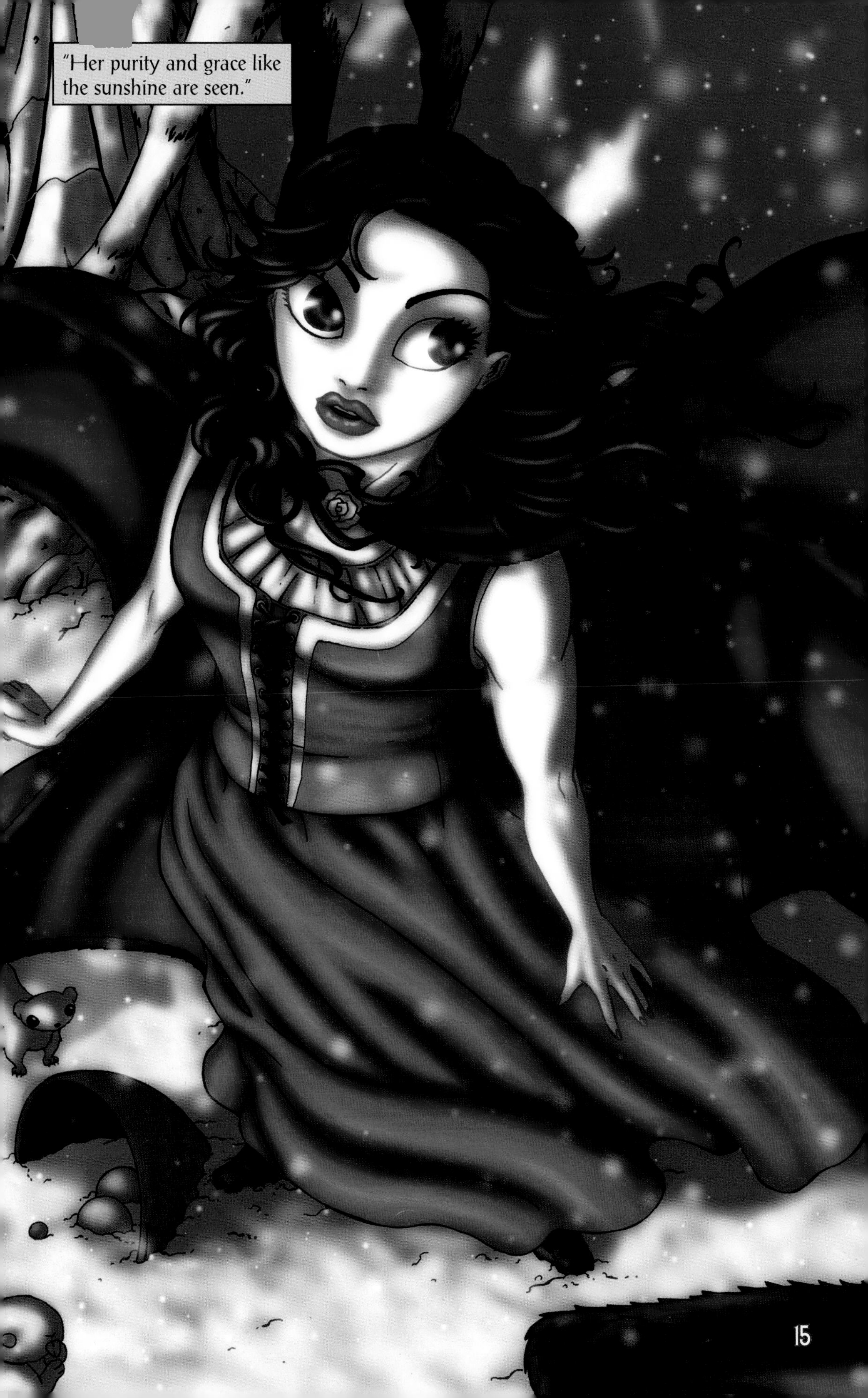
"Her purity and grace like the sunshine are seen."

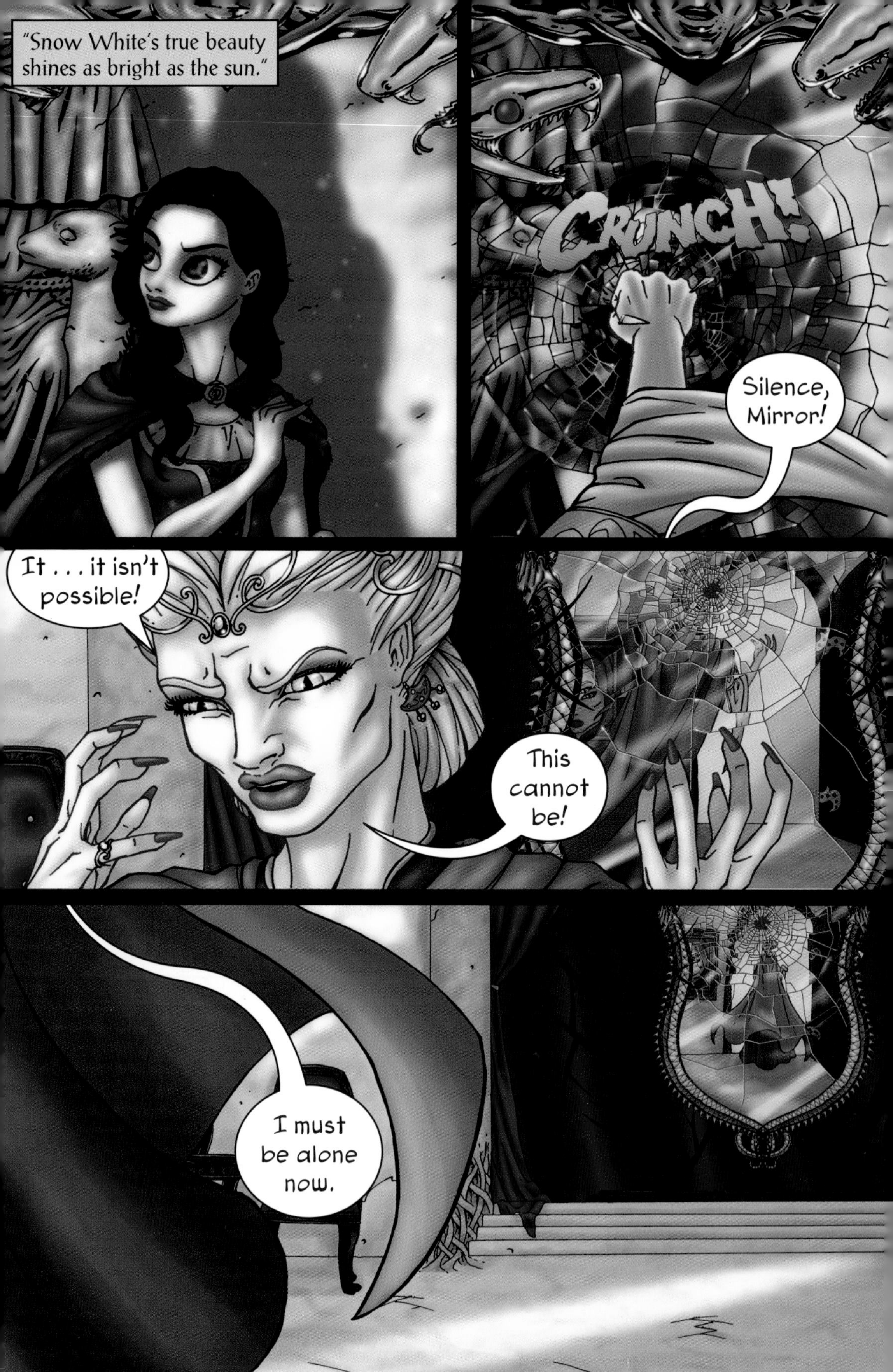
"Snow White's true beauty shines as bright as the sun."
CRUNCH!
Silence, Mirror!
It . . . it isn't possible!
This cannot be!
I must be alone now.

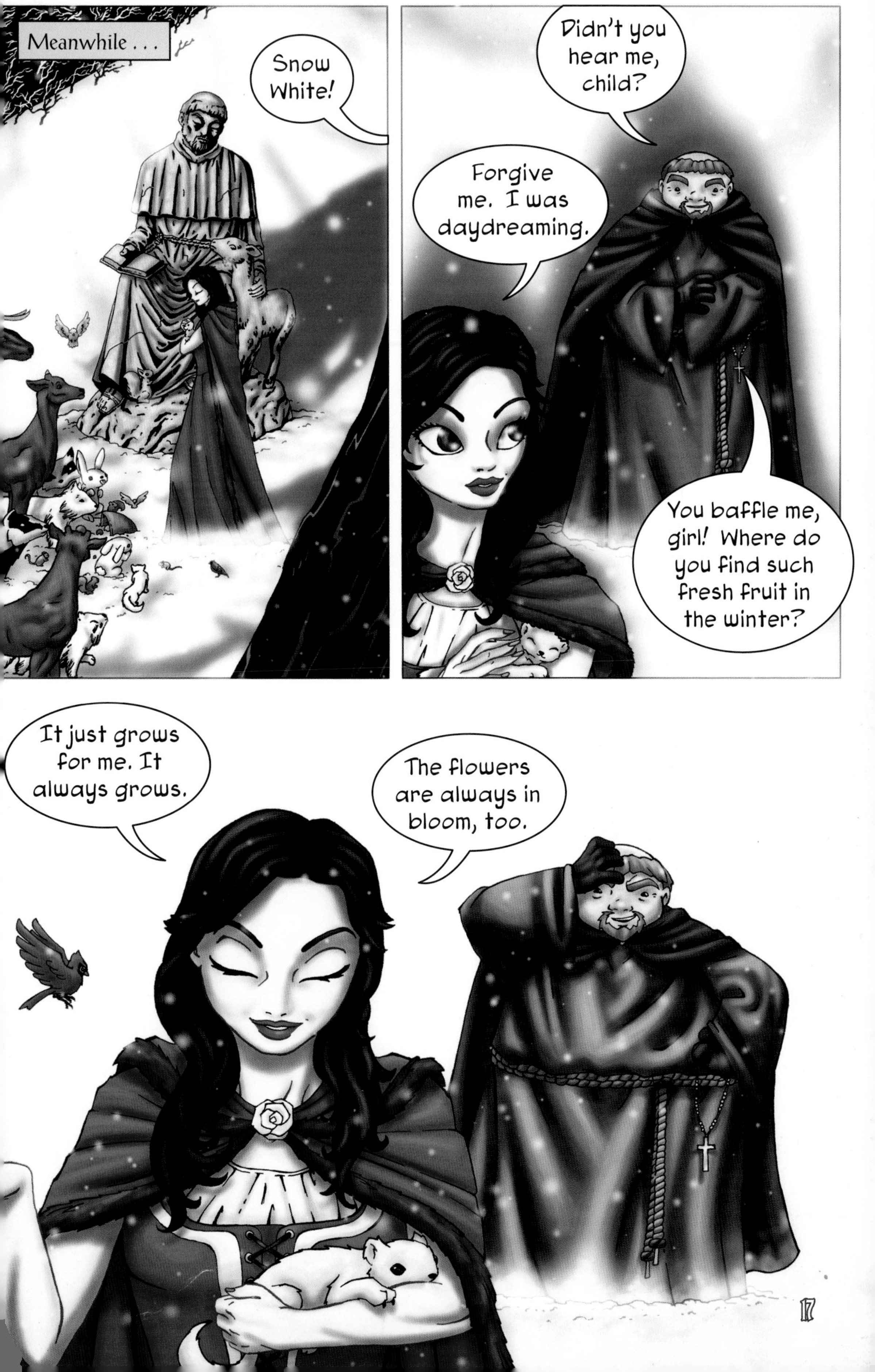
Meanwhile . . .
Snow White!
Didn't you hear me, child?
Forgive me. I was daydreaming.
You baffle me, girl! Where do you find such fresh fruit in the winter?
It just grows for me. It always grows.
The flowers are always in bloom, too.

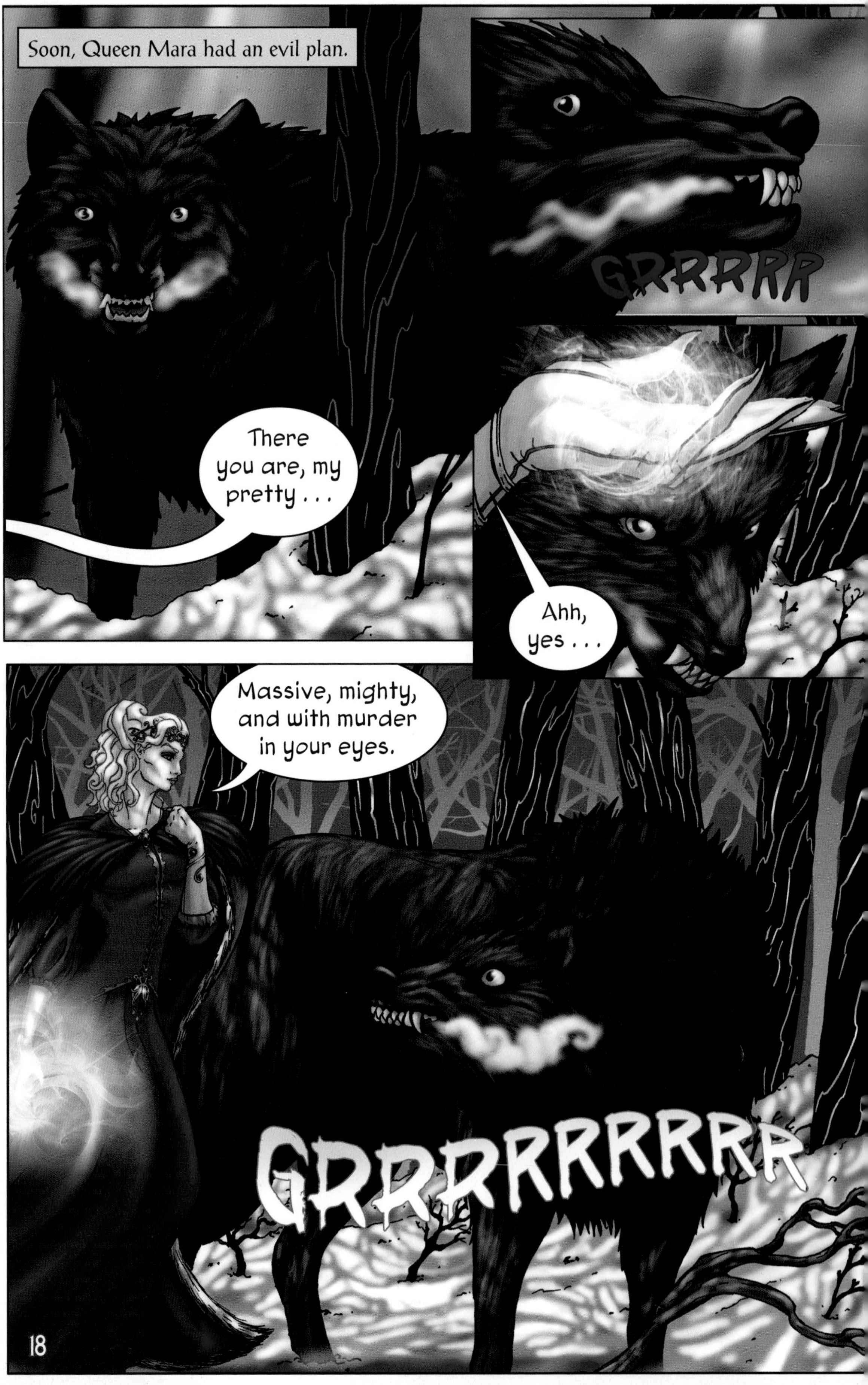
Soon, Queen Mara had an evil plan.
GRRRRR
There you are, my pretty . . .
Ahh, yes . . .
Massive, mighty, and with murder in your eyes.
GRRRRRRRRR

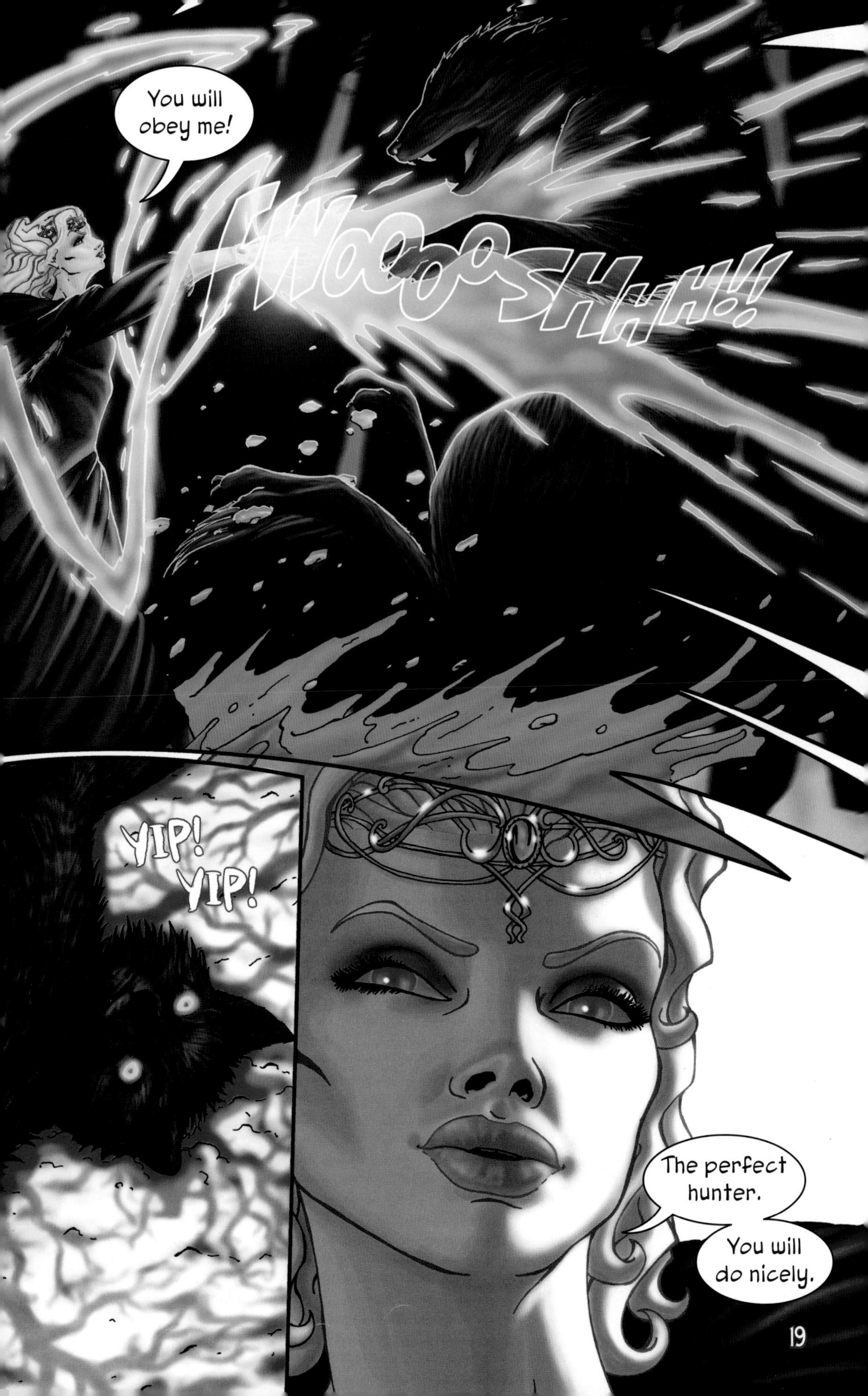
You will obey me!
FWOOOOSHHH!!
YIP! YIP!
The perfect hunter.
You will do nicely.

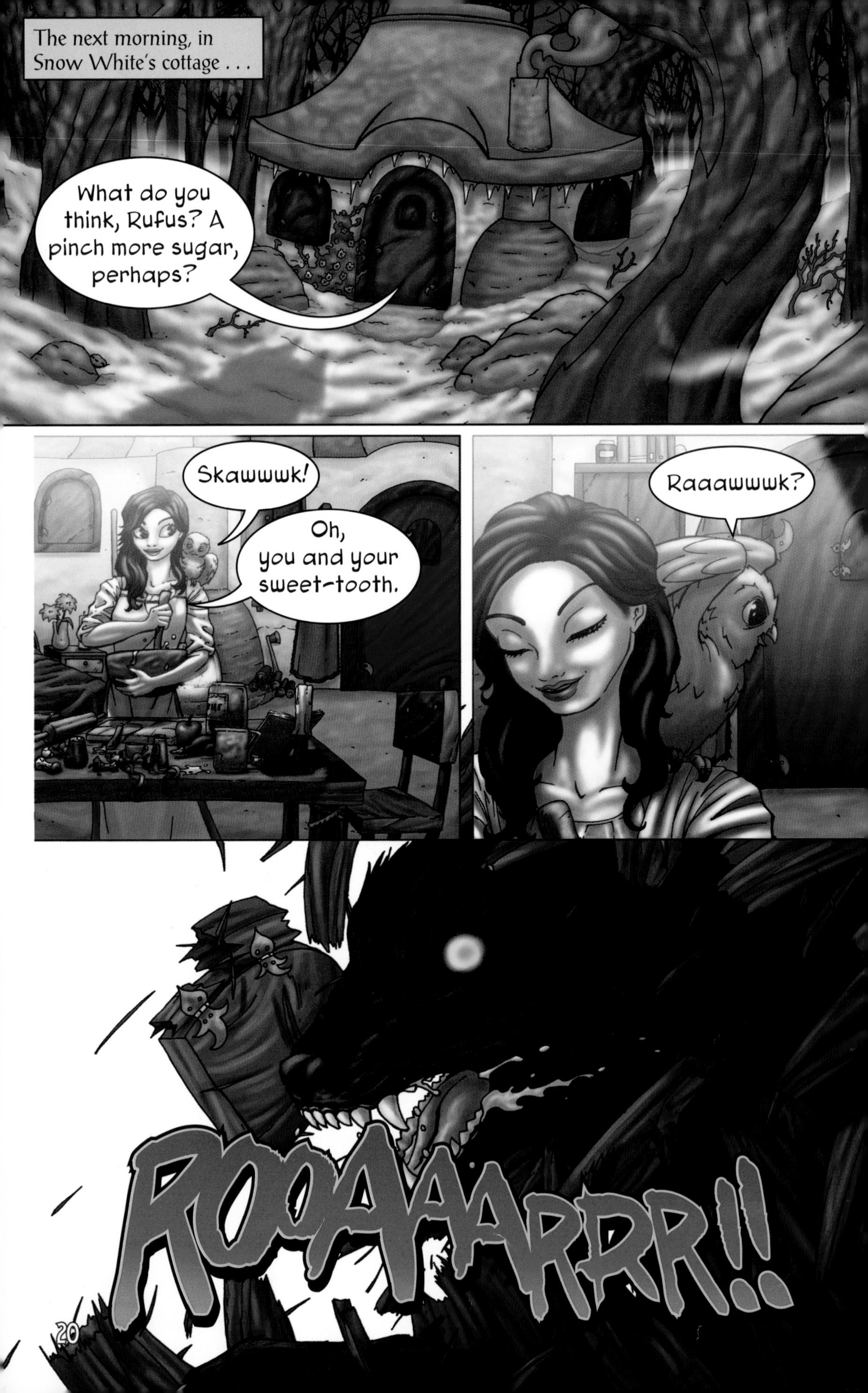
The next morning, in Snow White's cottage . . .
What do you think, Rufus? A pinch more sugar, perhaps?
Skawwwk!
Oh, you and your sweet-tooth.
Raaawwwk?
ROOAAARRR!!

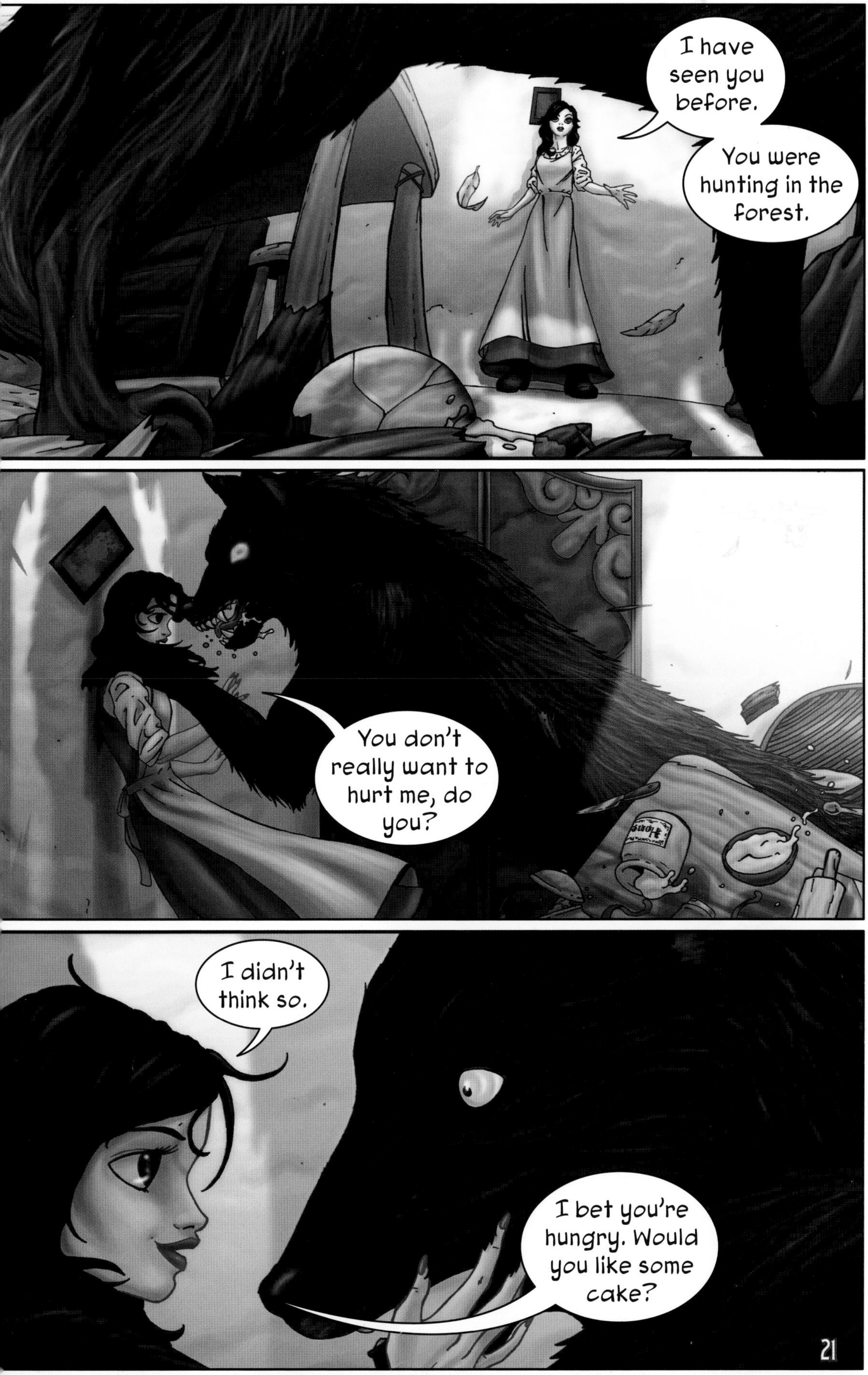
I have seen you before.
You were hunting in the forest.
You don't really want to hurt me, do you?
I didn't think so.
I bet you're hungry. Would you like some cake?

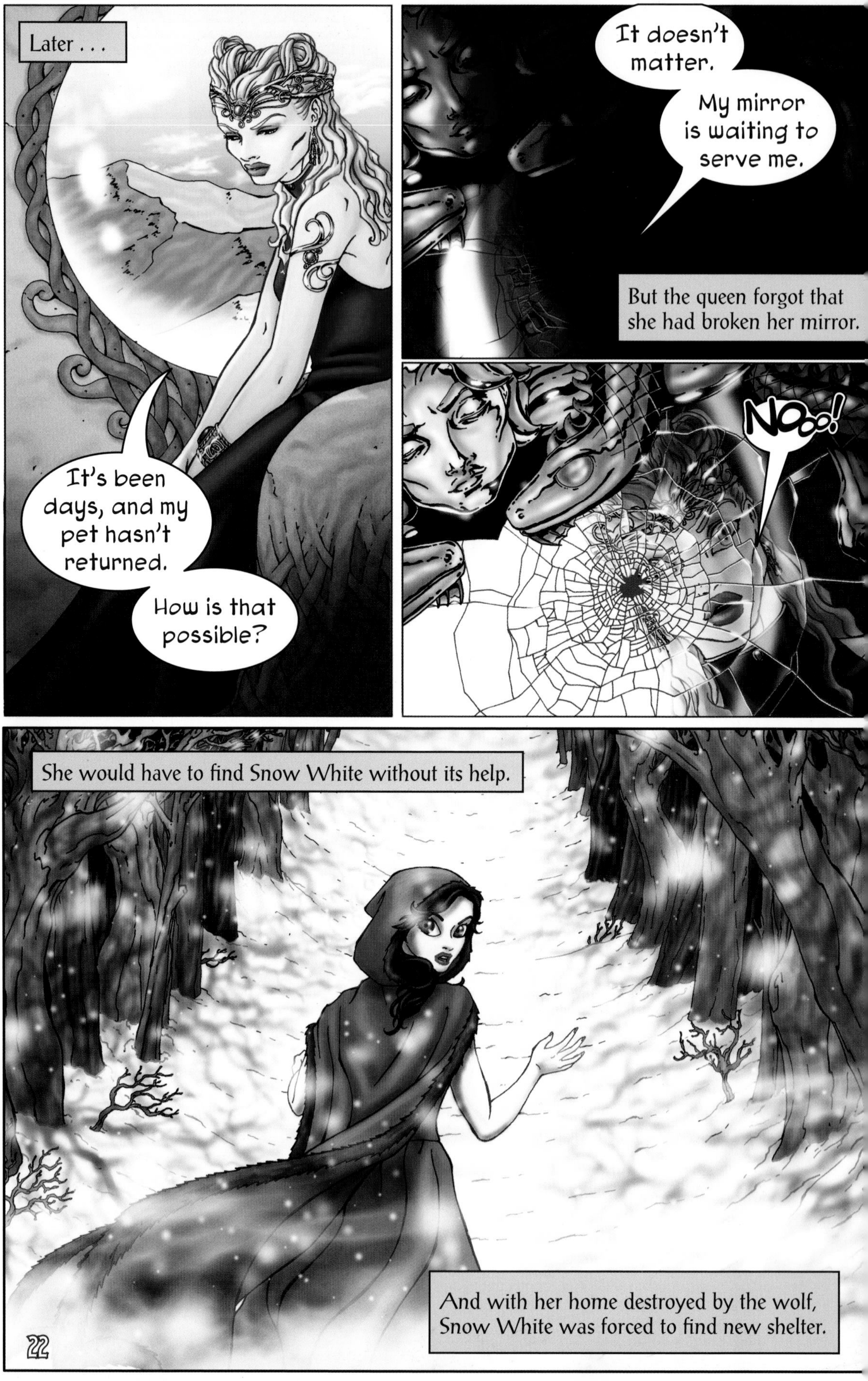
Later . . .
It's been days, and my pet hasn't returned.
How is that possible?
It doesn't matter.
My mirror is waiting to serve me.
But the queen forgot that she had broken her mirror.
NOoo!
She would have to find Snow White without its help.
And with her home destroyed by the wolf, Snow White was forced to find new shelter.

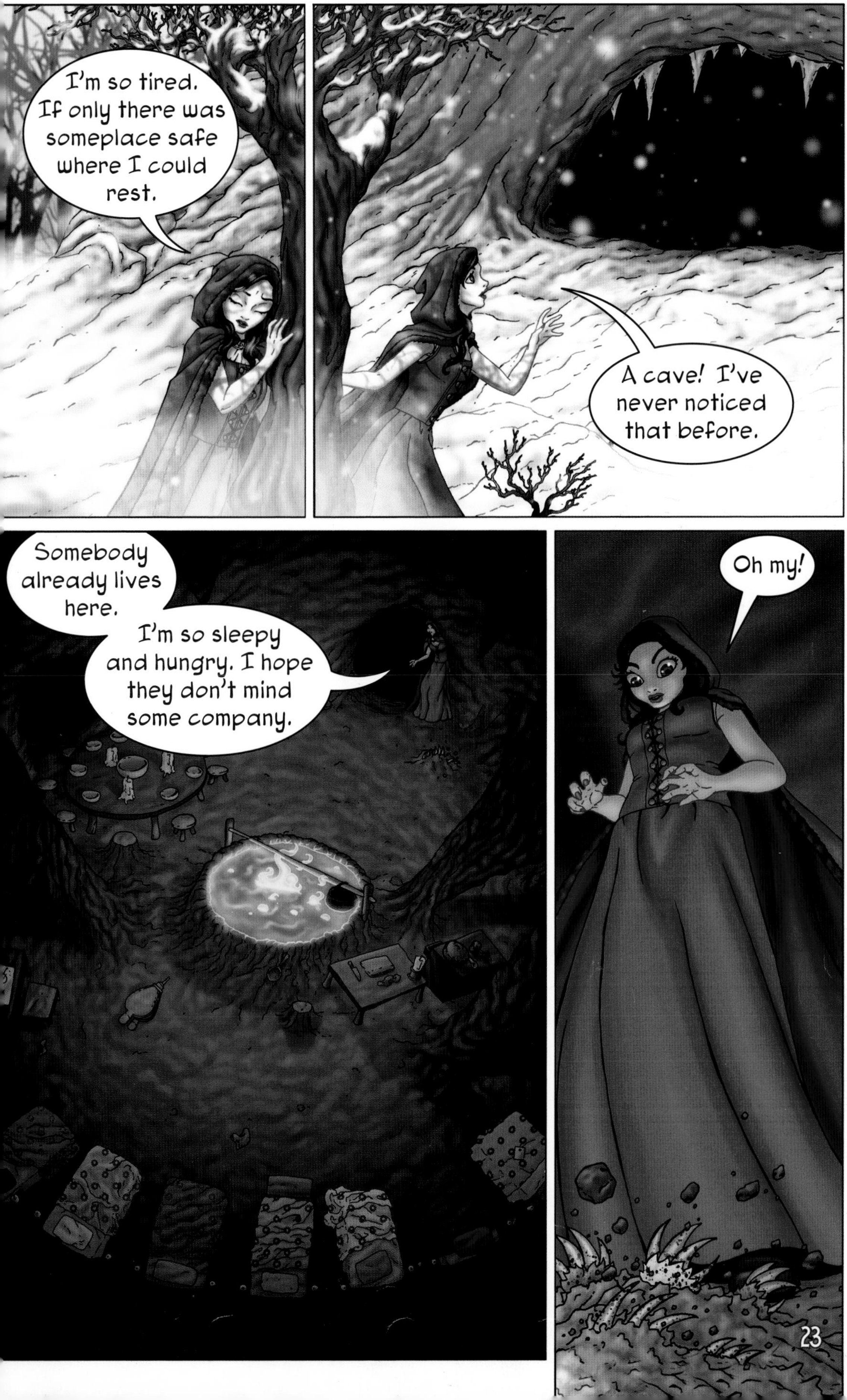
I'm so tired. If only there was someplace safe where I could rest.
A cave! I've never noticed that before.
Somebody already lives here.
I'm so sleepy and hungry. I hope they don't mind some company.
Oh my!

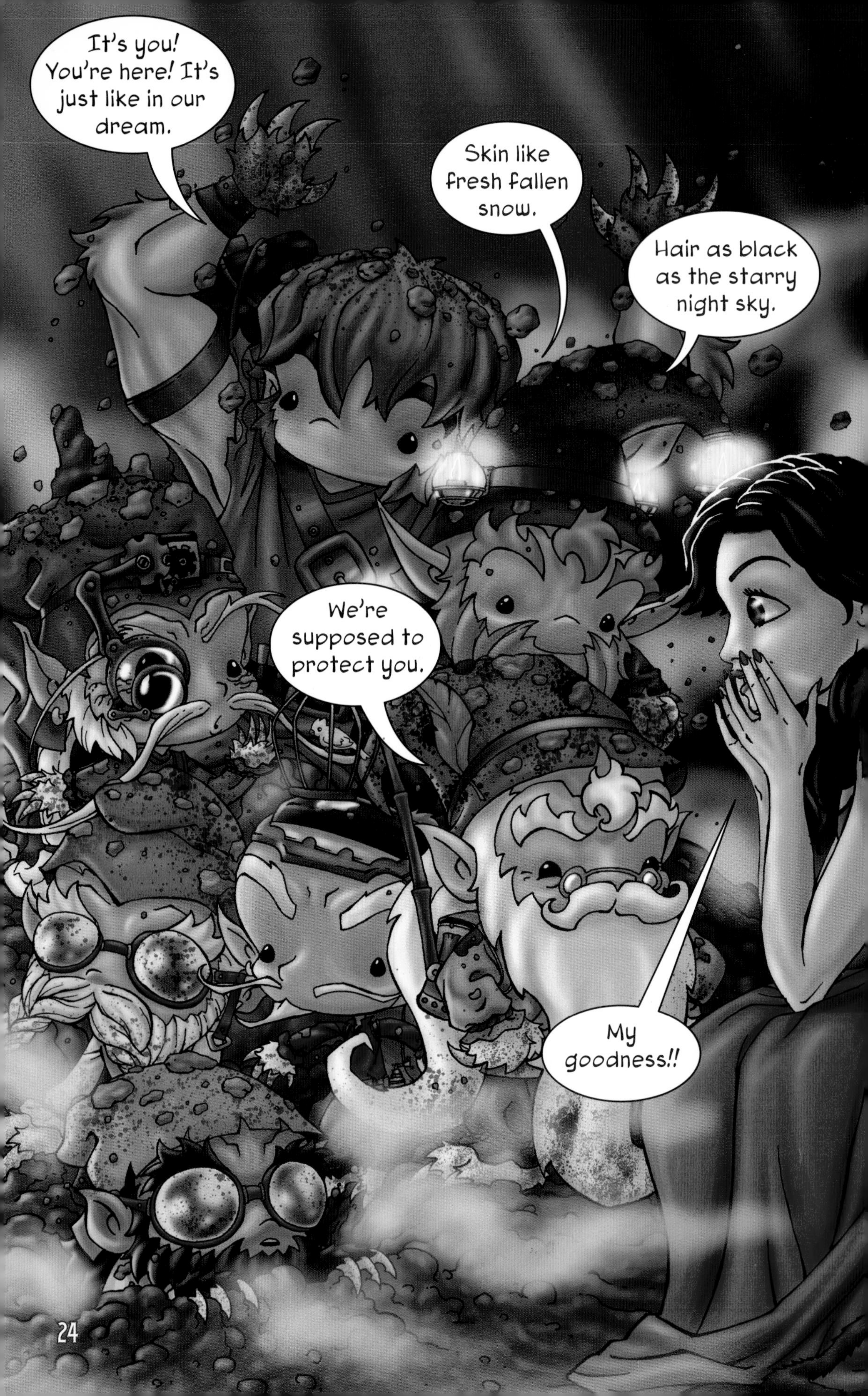
It's you! You're here! It's just like in our dream.
Skin like fresh fallen snow.
Hair as black as the starry night sky.
We're supposed to protect you.
My goodness!!

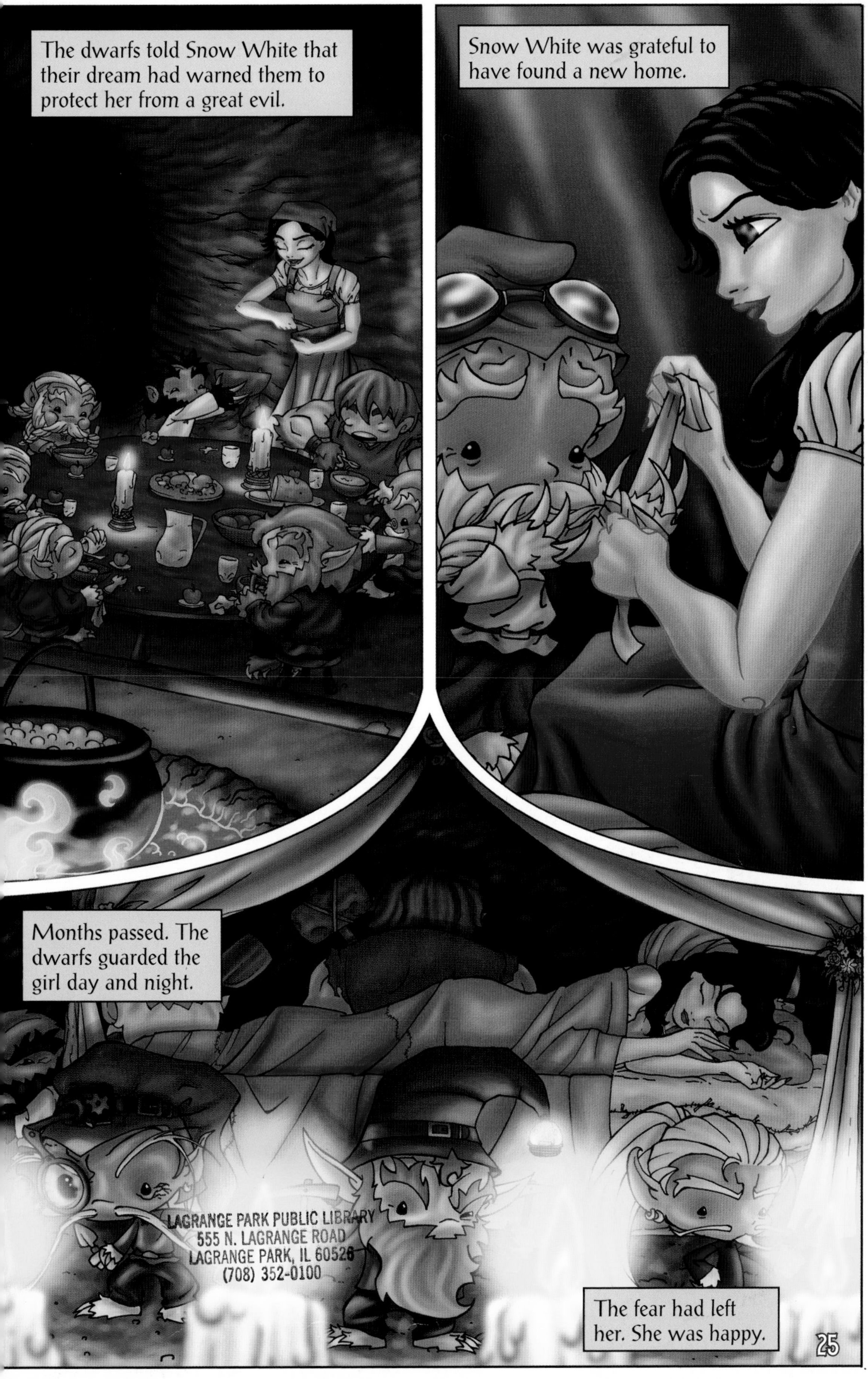
The dwarfs told Snow White that their dream had warned them to protect her from a great evil.
Snow White was grateful to have found a new home.
Months passed. The dwarfs guarded the girl day and night.
The fear had left her. She was happy.

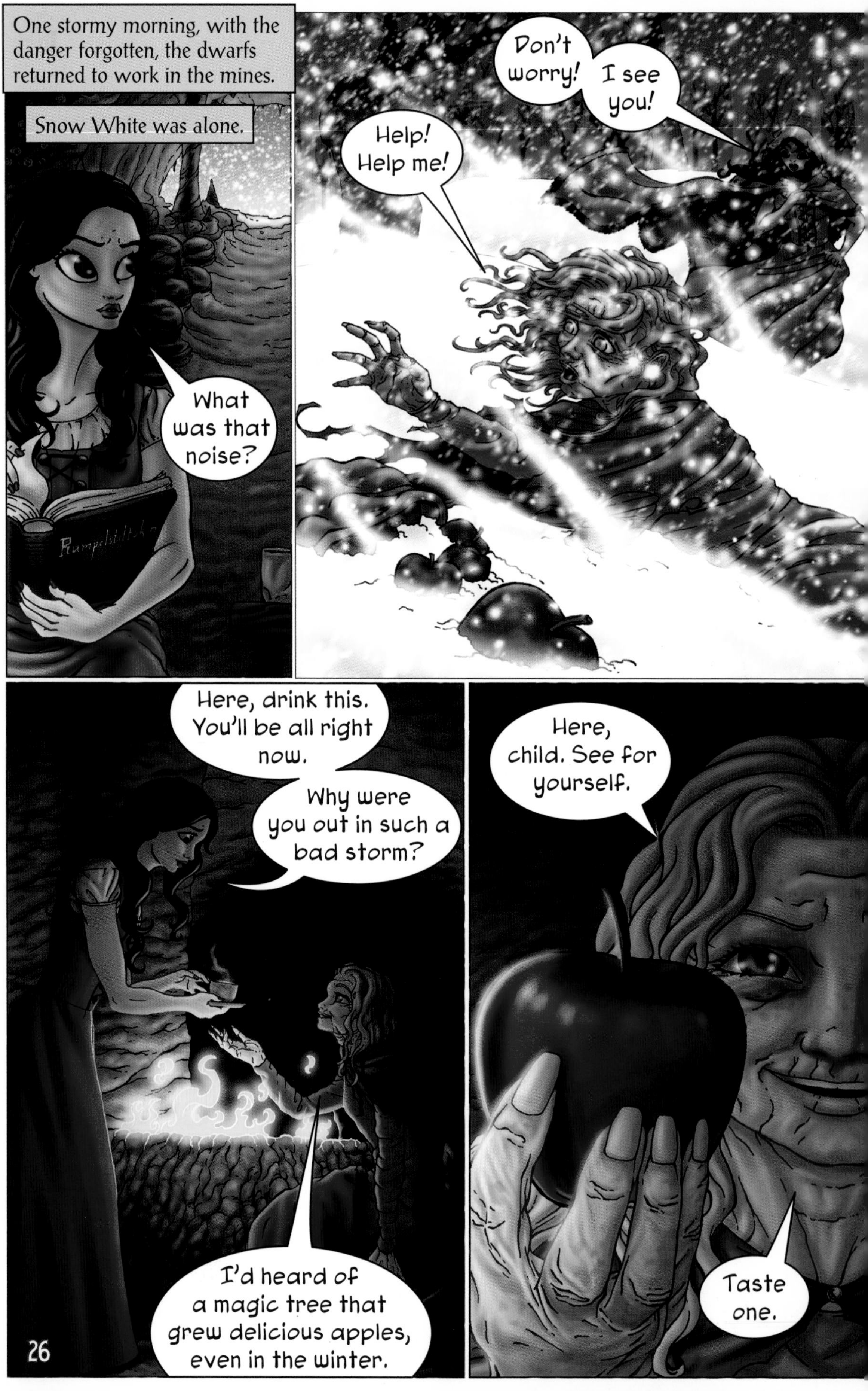

One stormy morning, with the danger forgotten, the dwarfs returned to work in the mines.
Snow White was alone.
What was that noise?
Rumpelstiltskin
Help! Help me!
Don't worry!
I see you!
Here, drink this. You'll be all right now.
Why were you out in such a bad storm?
I'd heard of a magic tree that grew delicious apples, even in the winter.
Here, child. See for yourself.
Taste one.

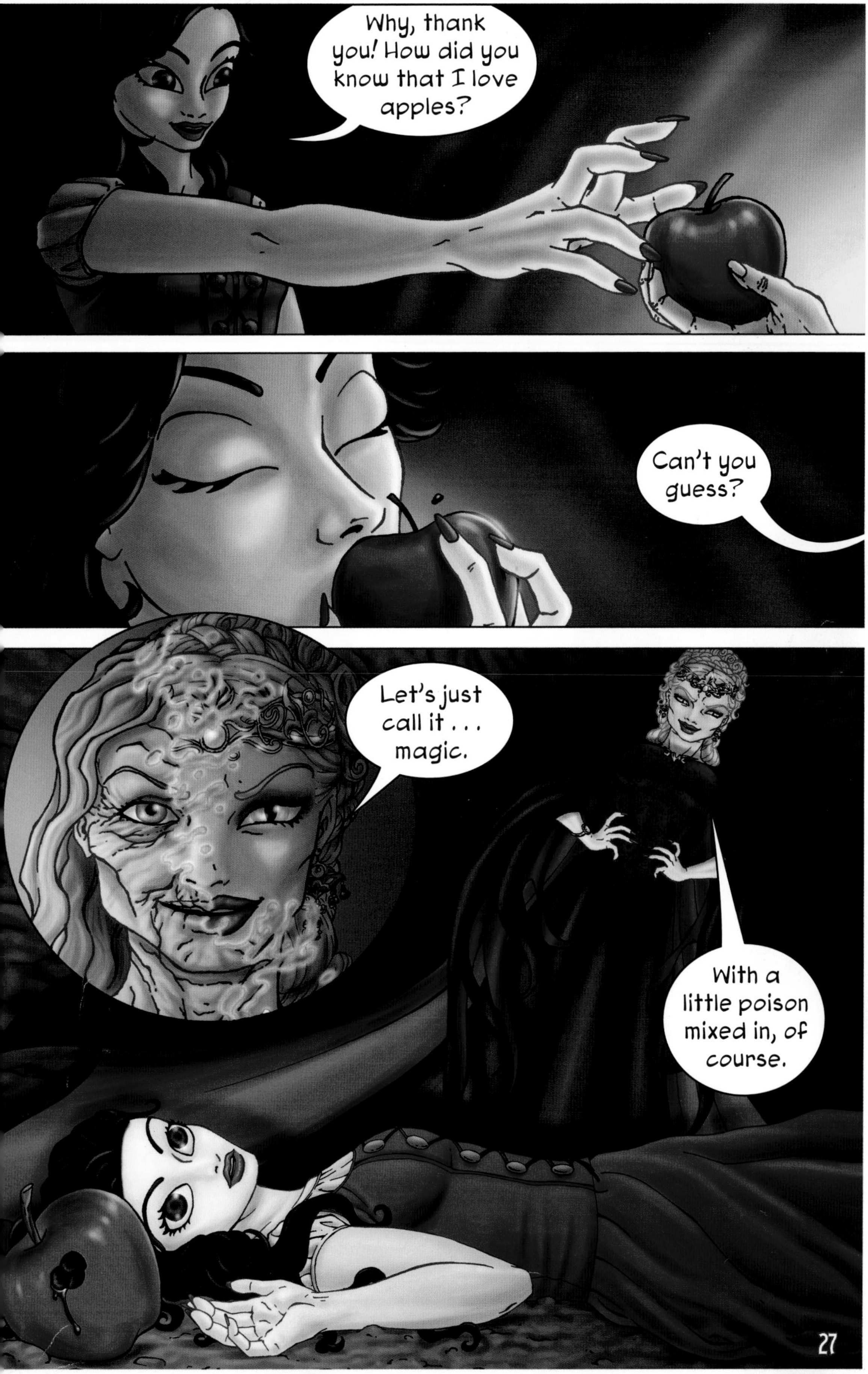
Why, thank you! How did you know that I love apples?
Can't you guess?
Let's just call it . . . magic.
With a little poison mixed in, of course.

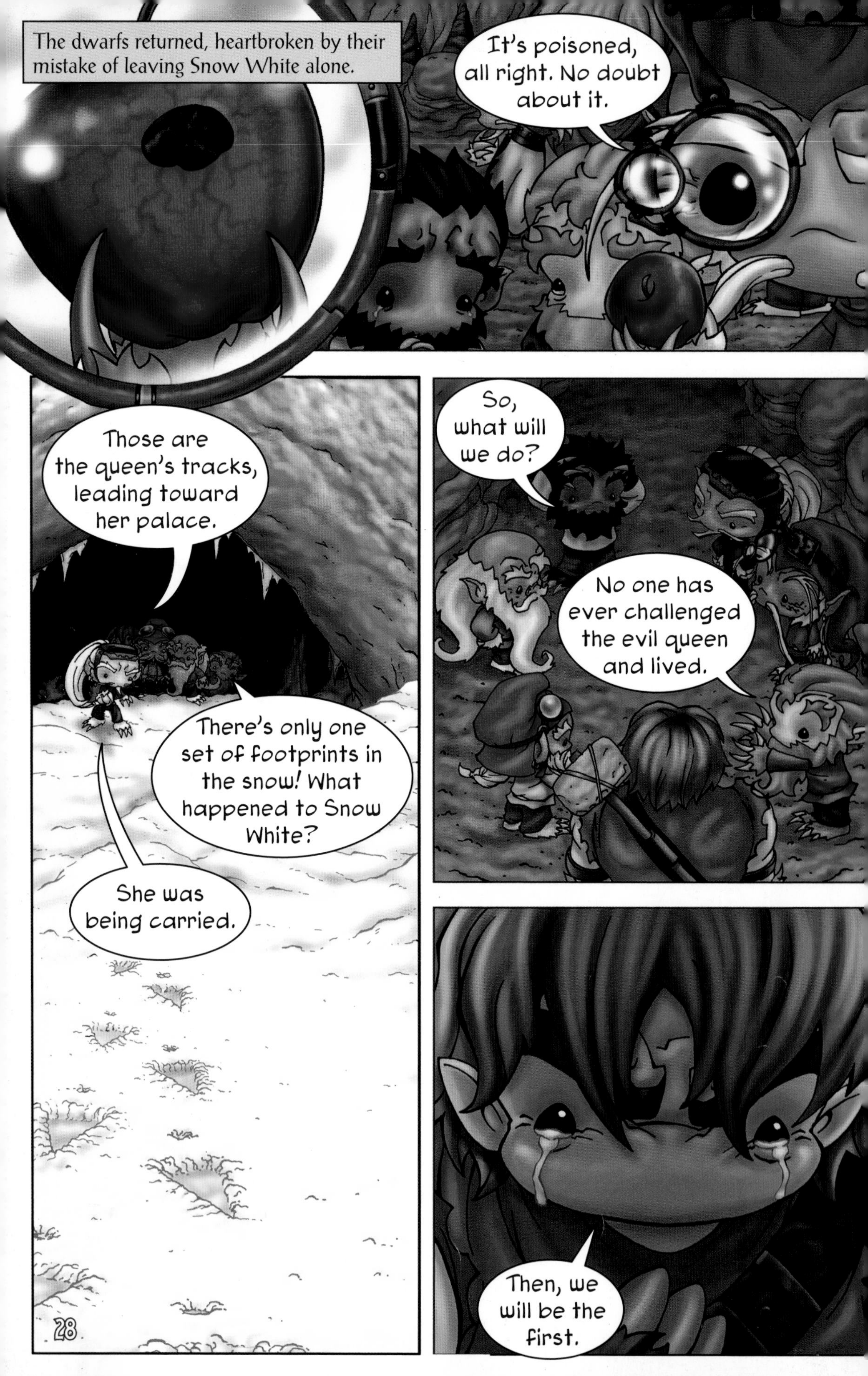

The dwarfs returned, heartbroken by their mistake of leaving Snow White alone.
It's poisoned, all right. No doubt about it.
Those are the queen's tracks, leading toward her palace.
There's only one set of footprints in the snow! What happened to Snow White?
She was being carried.
So, what will we do?
No one has ever challenged the evil queen and lived.
Then, we will be the first.

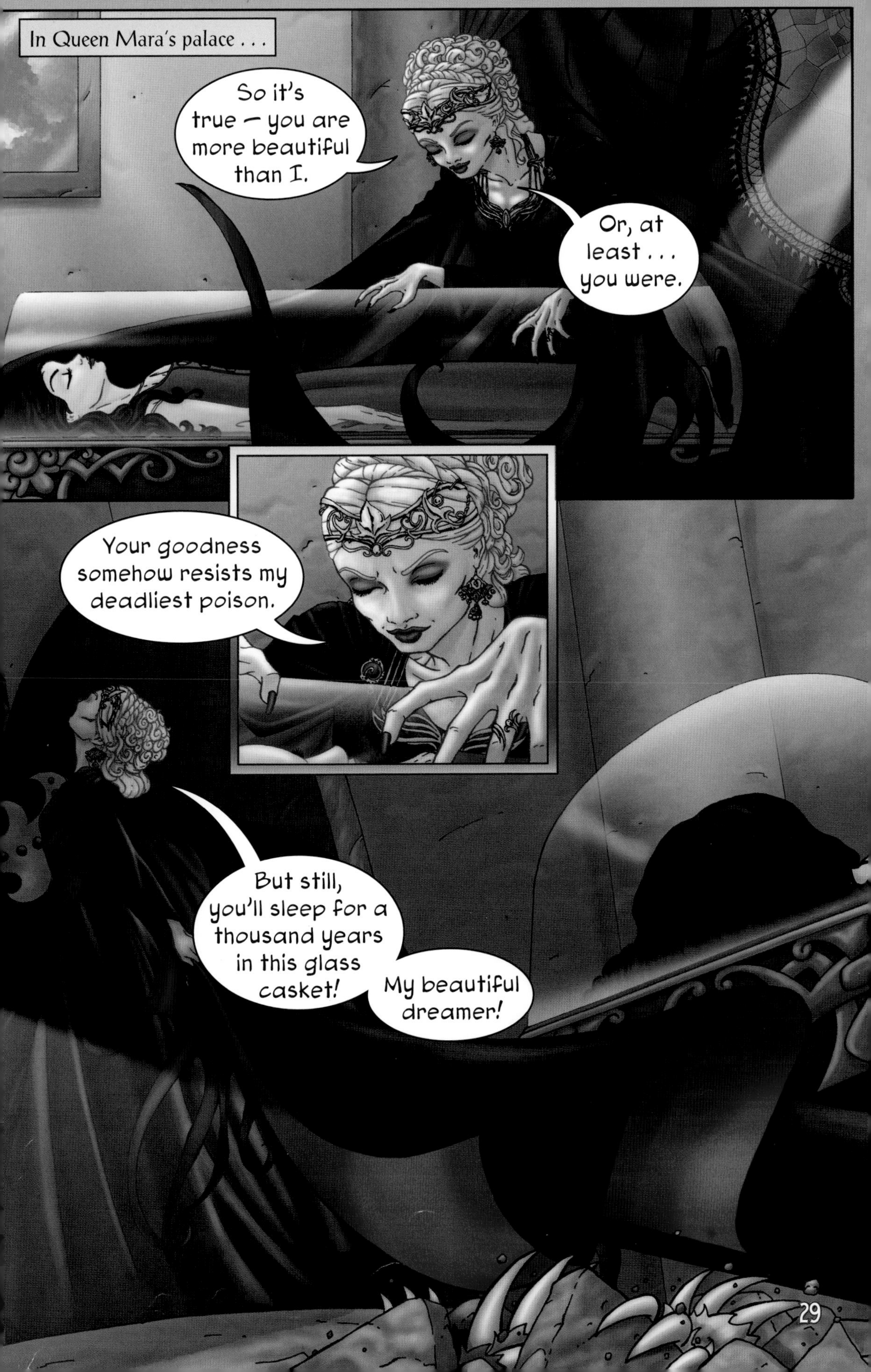
In Queen Mara's palace . . .
So it's true — you are more beautiful than I.
Or, at least . . . you were.
Your goodness somehow resists my deadliest poison.
But still, you'll sleep for a thousand years in this glass casket!
My beautiful dreamer!

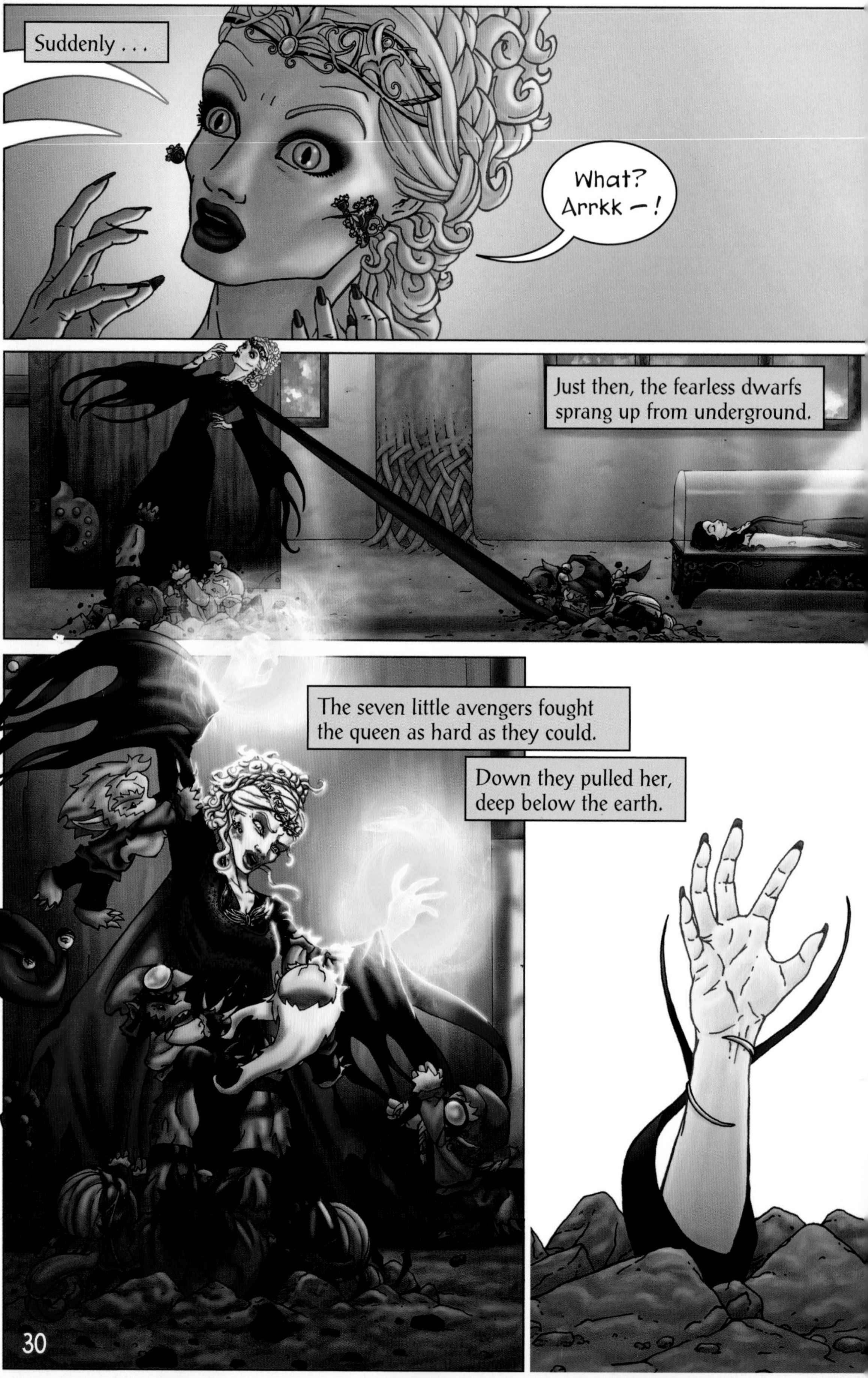
Suddenly . . .
What? Arrkk —!
Just then, the fearless dwarfs sprang up from underground.
The seven little avengers fought the queen as hard as they could.
Down they pulled her, deep below the earth.

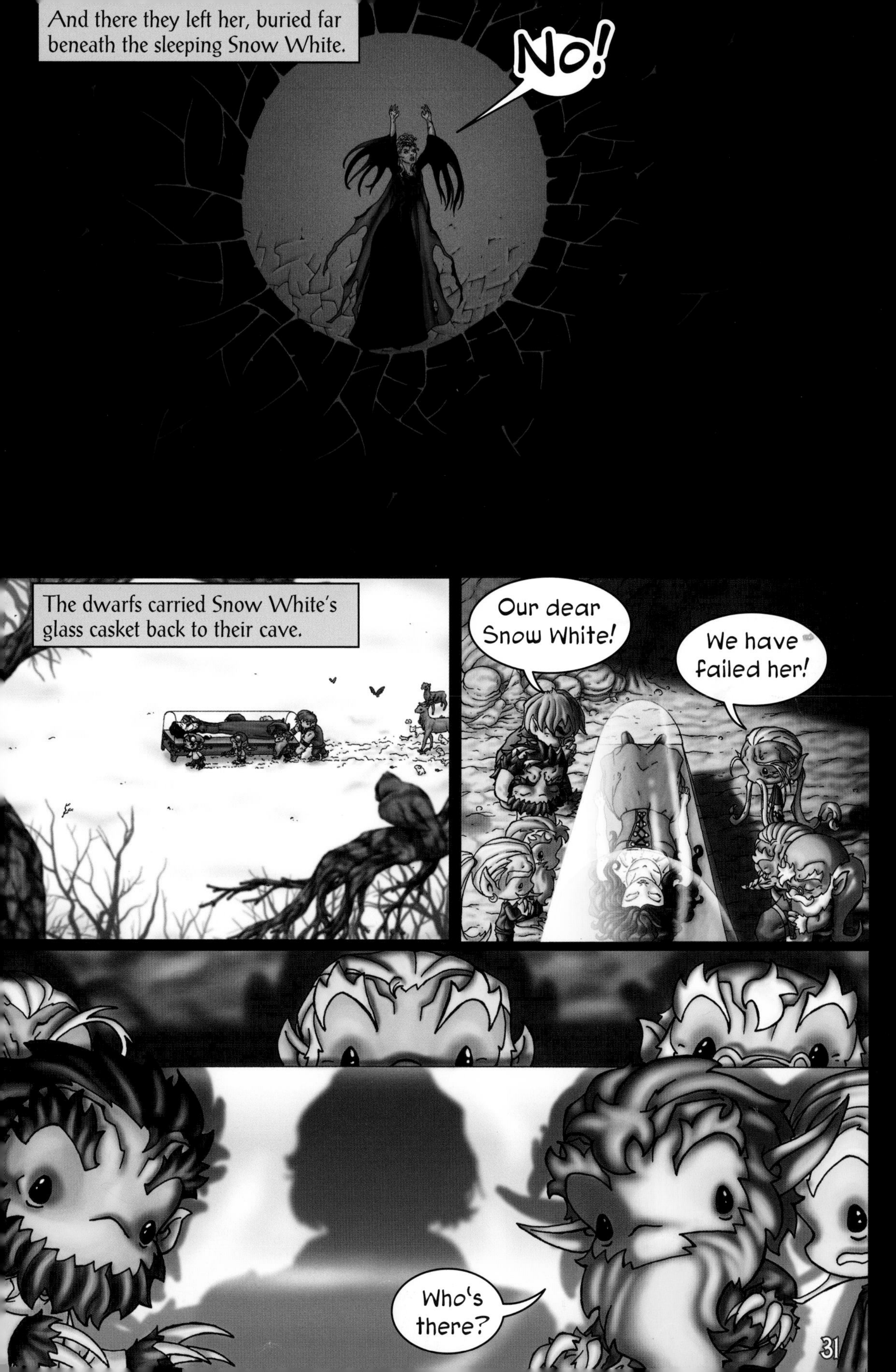
And there they left her, buried far beneath the sleeping Snow White.
No!
The dwarfs carried Snow White's glass casket back to their cave.
Our dear Snow White!
We have failed her!
Who's there?

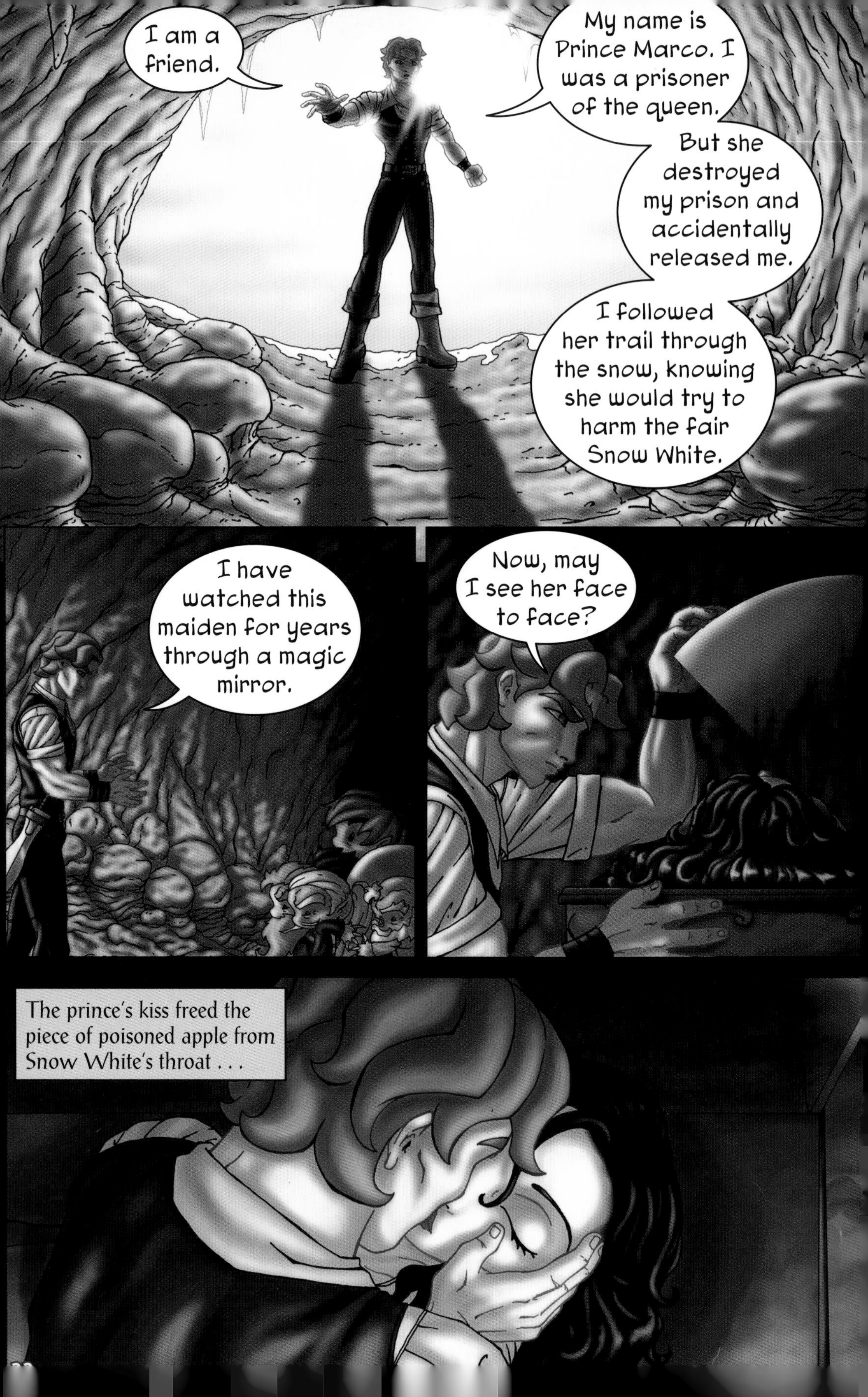
I am a friend.
My name is Prince Marco. I was a prisoner of the queen.
But she destroyed my prison and accidentally released me.
I followed her trail through the snow, knowing she would try to harm the fair Snow White.
I have watched this maiden for years through a magic mirror.
Now, may I see her face to face?
The prince's kiss freed the piece of poisoned apple from Snow White's throat . . .

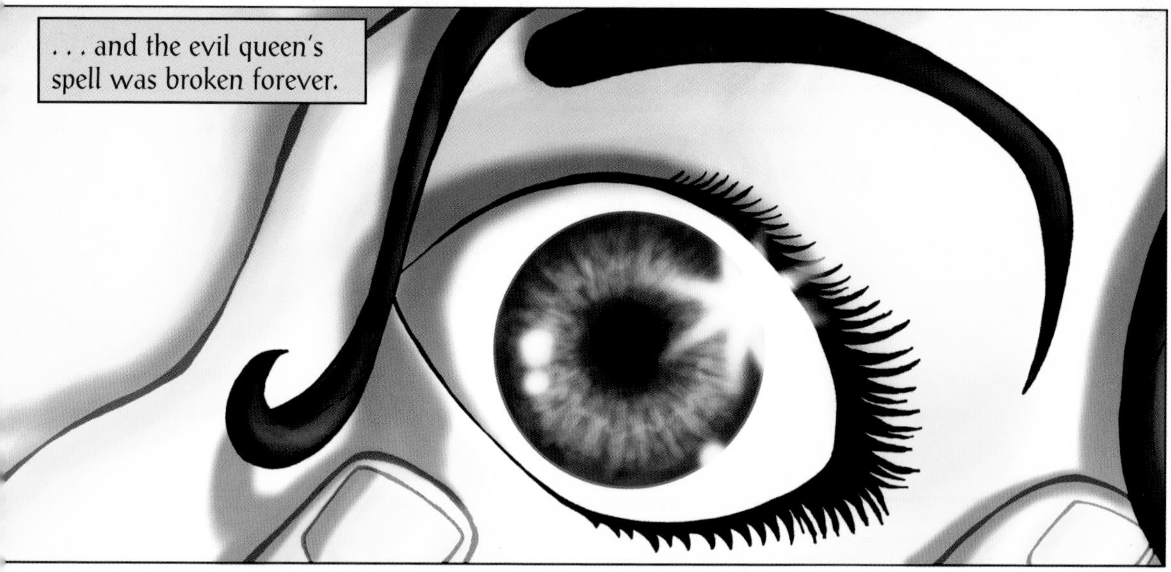
. . . and the evil queen's
spell was broken forever.

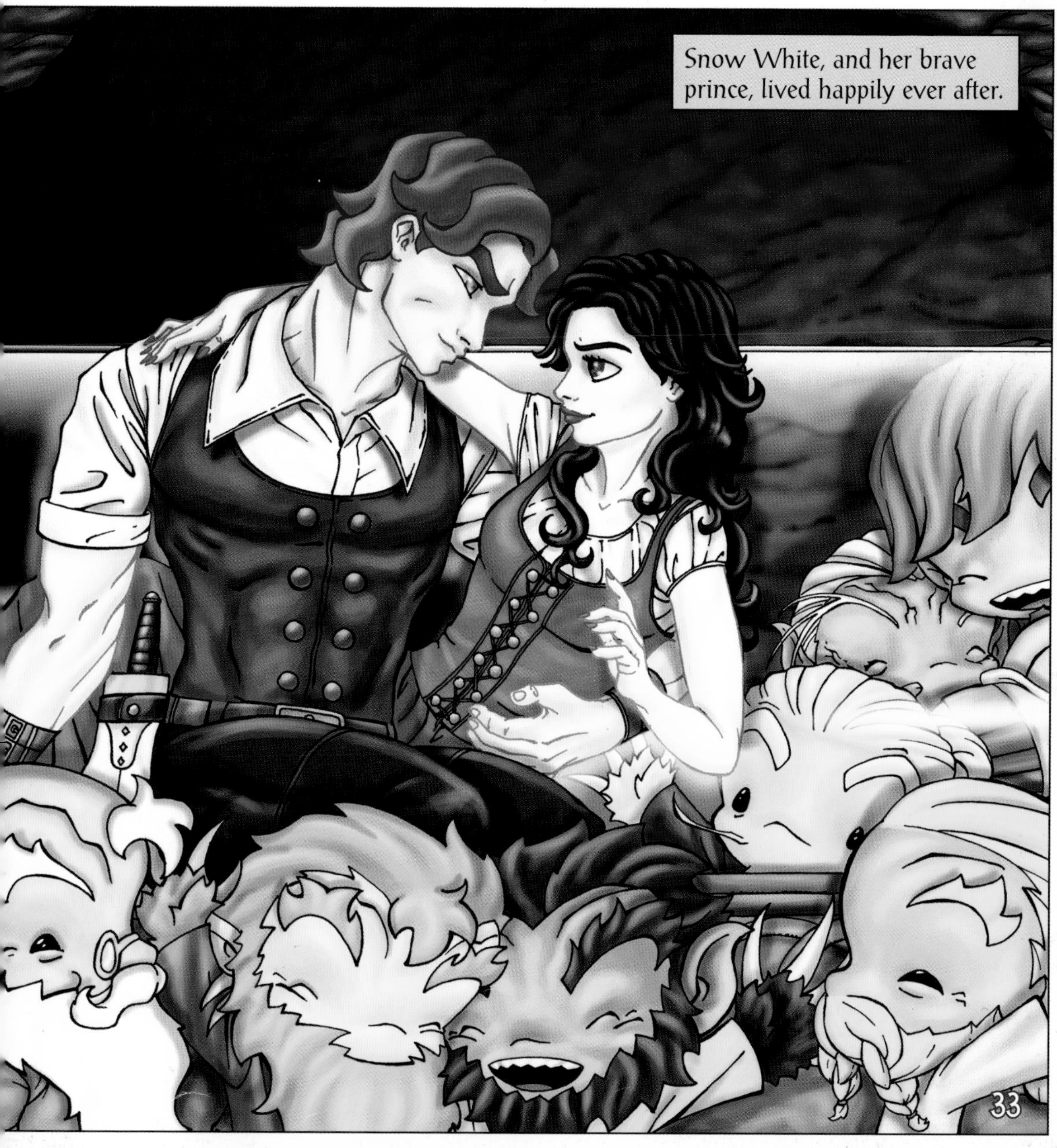
Snow White, and her brave
prince, lived happily ever after.

About the Author

Since 1986, Martin Powell has been a freelance writer. He has written hundreds of stories, many of which have been published by Disney, Marvel, Tekno comic, Moonstone Books, and others. In 1989, Powell received an Eisner Award nomination for his graphic novel *Scarlet in Gaslight*. This award is one of the highest comic book honors.

About the Illustrator

Erik Valdez y Alanis was born and raised in Mexico City, Mexico, and has been drawing since age 2. He uses his passion for art for illustrating, painting, and design work. Valdez has won a number of awards for his art including the L. Ron Hubbard Gold Award for Illustrator of the Future in 2004. He has done illustrations for books, magazines, and CD covers. Today, Valdez has focused on comics including, most recently, *The Sleepy Truth* for Viper Comics. When he's not working, Valdez loves traveling, really good books, and chocolate cake.

Glossary

avenger (uh-VEHNJ-uhr)—someone who gets revenge

baffle (BAF-uhl)—to puzzle or confuse someone

casket (KASS-kit)—a long container in which a dead person is placed for burial

cruel (KROO-uhl)—mean or unfair

grateful (GRAYT-fuhl)—thankful

handsome (HAN-suhm)—attractive in appearance

maiden (MAYD-uhn)—a young and unmarried woman

shelter (SHEL-tur)—a place to keep covered in bad weather or safe and protected from danger

THE HISTORY OF
SNOW WHITE

Stories similar to "Snow White" are found in cultures throughout the world. Some details of the centuries-old tale vary, according to location. A Scottish version, for example, has a talking fish in a well rather than a magic mirror.

Like many fairy tales, the most well-known version comes from the Brothers Grimm. Jacob and Wilhelm Grimm were German brothers who published collections of oral fairy tales in the 1800s. Family friends Jeannette and Amalie Hassenpflug told the Grimm brothers the story. Many of the details of the sisters' story were similar to Italian versions. The dwarfs, however, must have been a German addition. German folk tales often include stocky little men who work underground.

The Grimm version of "Snow White" was used as the basis for the 1937 Walt Disney movie, *Snow White and the Seven Dwarfs*. It was the first American full-length animated movie.

For many people, the name Snow White brings to mind Happy, Grumpy, and Dopey. But these dwarf names, along with Doc, Sneezy, Sleepy, and Bashful, were never part of the original versions of the fairy tale. The movie is credited with naming the dwarfs and giving them personalities. The seven names were picked from a list of 50 possibilities, including Awful, Dirty, and Hoppy.

Some historians think that Snow White was based on a real person. Margaret von Waldeck lived in Germany in the 1500s, 200 years before the Grimm brothers were born. She lived in a mining town, was loved by a handsome prince, Phillip II of Spain, and was poisoned at the early age of 21. The villain was never found.

DISCUSSION QUESTIONS

1. Why was it so important to the queen that she was the most beautiful person in the world? What does this say about her character?

2. When Snow White discovered the "old woman" who was in trouble, she rushed to help her. What does this say about Snow White's character? Compare and contrast her character with the queen's character.

3. Fairy tales are often told over and over again. Have your heard the "Snow White" fairy tale before? How is this version of the story different from other versions you've heard, seen, or read?

WRITING PROMPTS

1. What if Snow White had lived with seven giants, rather than seven dwarfs? What sort of home would they have had? Describe this new setting.

2. The dwarfs felt responsible for watching over Snow White, but they could not watch her during the day when they were at work. Write a list of rules for Snow White to follow when she was home alone.

3. The story ends by saying that Snow White and her prince lived happily ever after. What about the dwarfs? Write a story about what happens to the little men. Do they join Snow White in her new home? Are they left to watch over another person in danger?

INTERNET SITES

The book may be over, but the adventure is just beginning.

Do you want to read more about the subjects or ideas in
this book? Want to play cool games or watch videos about
the authors who write these books? Then go to **FactHound**.
At *www.facthound.com*, you'll be able to do all that, and
more. The FactHound website can also send you to other
safe Internet sites.

Check it out!